One Thing I'm Good At

ONE THING I'M GOOD AT

KAREN LYNN WILLIAMS

SCHOLASTIC INC.
New York Toronto London Auckland Sydney
Mexico City New Delhi Hong Kong

ISBN 0-439-20912-9

Published by Scholastic Inc., 555 Broadway, New York, NY 10012,
by arrangement with Lothrop, Lee & Shepard, a division of
William Morrow & Company, Inc.

12 11 10 9 8 7 6 5 4 3 2 1 0 1 2 3 4 5/0

Printed in the U.S.A. 40

First Scholastic printing, September 2000

For Rachel, a very special daughter, who is more than good at many things.

One Thing I'm Good At

One

"PAPER, SCISSORS, ROCK." Julie held her hand out flat, palm up.

Bean shot out two small fingers in a V. "I win," he said. "Scissors cut paper. Let's do it again." He shoved his pudgy fist behind his back.

"Okay." Julie sighed and pushed her straggly brown hair over her ear. They sat on the floor of the bedroom she shared with her younger brother. "But this is the last time." She really didn't like the game. It was boring and she always felt funny about the idea of it, the idea of power, that scissors cut paper and a rock can crush scissors. She was probably the only kid in the whole world who thought about dumb stuff like that. She placed her fist behind her back. "Ready?"

Bean smiled. His shiny black hair bounced up and down as he nodded. His eyes twinkled with anticipation. Dad had taught Julie and their older sister, Alexia, the game before Bean was even born. Now Julie was teaching Bean. He was only four, but he was real smart for his age. He learned the game in about two seconds. Bean had memorized their telephone number and address and he knew the whole alphabet and how to count to twenty.

It had been about twenty minutes since Dad left for his doctor's appointment and Julie was babysitting. Real baby-sitting. Alexia was due home soon, but for now Julie was the one in charge.

"Paper, scissors, rock." Julie made a V this time.

"I win." Bean yelled as he held out a tight little fist. "Rock crushes scissors." He giggled with excitement.

Bean was always happy. Must be because he never had homework. But Julie did. She had to get started before Mom and Dad got home. Two "poor work" papers again today! If she started her homework without being told, maybe they wouldn't think so much about the two D papers that had to be signed. She didn't want to upset Mom or Dad. Especially Dad. Julie didn't want to do anything that might excite him. Back in September, Dad had had a heart attack. Before that, he was a firefighter. Now he stayed home and Mom worked as a secretary. Julie's stomach began to knot up the way it did every time she thought about how her father's heart had just stopped without any warning. He was better now and studying for a new job with computers, but Julie still worried.

"Okay, Bean, you find something to do. I have to get to work." She stood up, groaning. Mean Mrs. Spattelli had given the blue reading group extra work just because no one knew the definition of *folly*. The other kids hadn't gotten any reading homework. It wasn't fair.

"Come on, Julie, one more time."

Julie dragged her backpack over to the desk. It felt like it was filled with rocks instead of homework. "As long as you promise not to ask again." She put her right hand behind her back.

"I promise." Bean sat at her feet.

"Well, come on. Get up." Julie tapped the fingers

of her left hand, clicking her nails on the desktop. She had math homework, too. And she had missed lunch recess today, all because of Mrs. Spattelli.

Just because she hadn't had time to finish her English assignment in class, "Mrs. Spit" made her do it during recess, and Julie had missed the marble tournament. She hadn't even had a chance to win her best shooter back from Brian. Just thinking about Mrs. Spit made Julie feel like hitting something. Ten, twenty, thirty . . . She tried counting by tens to calm herself.

Bean stood up. His right hand was behind his back.

"Paper, scissors, rock." Bean held out a flat hand. Paper.

Still thinking about sitting in that hot classroom when the other kids were outside, Julie curled her fingers into a tight fist. Rock. She pounded her fist down right on Bean's outstretched hand, smacking it into the desk.

"Ouch! Julie! What did you do that for?" Tears welled up in Bean's big brown eyes.

Julie didn't know why she had done it. But she remembered Alexia used to do it to her all the time. "Don't be such a baby."

Bean sniffed. "Rock doesn't even beat paper." The tears rolled down his cheeks.

"Come on, Bean. I told you I have work to do. I played with you enough. Now you keep yourself busy. Go on over to your desk. You can pretend you're at school. Real school." Bean went to day care three days a week while Dad took his computer classes.

Julie watched her brother inch over to his side of the room. She used to share a room with Alexia, but now Alexia had moved into the small room that used to be Bean's and Bean had moved in with Julie. Julie didn't mind sharing with her brother. At least now *she* got to make the rules about the room and had the side with the windows. Dad was supposed to move the bookcases and Mom was going to put up a curtain to divide the room. They already had the fabric. Julie had picked it out. But that was before Dad's heart attack. He couldn't move heavy things now and Mom didn't have time to sew.

"Julie." Bean's voice was whiny. It came from right behind her, on her side of the room.

"Beeean!"

He just stood there.

"Look, I'll show you how to write *Benjamin*

Dorinsky and you can practice." Benjamin was Bean's real name. When he was born, Julie couldn't pronounce Benjamin. She called him Bean, and the name stuck. She had taught him how to write *Benjamin* weeks ago, and he did great. Now his day-care teacher wanted him to practice his full name.

Bean was still sniffling. He stuck out his lip. "I don't want to."

"Come on, Bean. I'm sorry I smacked your hand. You can use my colored pencils."

"Really?"

Julie knew that was a mistake, but she didn't care right then. She grabbed the pencils out of her desk drawer and tossed them on Bean's desk. They were real artist's pencils.

"Sure, you can draw a picture of our new room, the way it's going to look when Mom and Dad fix it up."

Bean's lower lip was still sticking out. "Julie, you bashed my hand." He rubbed his eyes with a tight little fist, leaving a dark smudge on his cheek.

"Look, Bean, I didn't mean to. I said I'm sorry."

Bean stared at her like he didn't believe it. Then he walked back to his side of the room, settled into his desk chair, and began removing the pencils from their box. One by one he named the colors, even chartreuse and burnt sienna, just as Julie had taught him.

Julie slumped back into her chair. She didn't know why she had pounded Bean like that. Today had been her first chance to really baby-sit and she had practically blown it.

Julie looked at the "poor work" papers. The last time she had papers to be signed, Mom and Dad ended up having a fight about who was going to talk to Mrs. Spit. That had been just last week.

She put her head down on the desk. She could hear Bean scribbling hard with one of her pencils, wearing down the point. It was a rotten day. School stunk. Mrs. Spit stunk. And she, Julie Dorinsky, was a dumb kid who couldn't do anything right.

Two

BRRRIIINNNG. JULIE JUMPED up from her desk, knocking her math and reading books on the floor. She had just gotten started on the first math problem, and there was the phone.

"The phone, Julie."

"I *know,* Bean." Julie stumbled over her backpack as she ran out of the room and downstairs. The kitchen phone was closer than the one in Mom and Dad's room on the third floor.

The portable phone wasn't there. Darn. It rang for the fourth time. Of course it was in Alexia's room. Alexia was always on the phone and she never put it back. Half the time the battery needed recharging. Julie ran upstairs and flung open Alexia's door. She nearly tripped over the tangle of her sister's overalls and sneakers. *Brrriiinnng.* It was definitely in here somewhere. Not on the desk. Not on the floor. One more ring and Dad's voice would come over the answering machine. "Hi! You have reached . . ." The next ring came from the bed, which was a mess of bedcovers, clothes, and books. Julie found a phone-shaped lump under the sheets. She grabbed for it and hit the on button just before the message began.

"Hello?"

"Hey, is Ali there?" The voice sounded distant, and there was music playing in the background.

"Who?" Julie asked before she realized they wanted Alexia. Ever since Alexia had started high school this year, she called herself Ali. Some of her new friends had started it. Figured it was one of her sister's friends that she had almost broken her neck for.

"She's not here."

"Could you please tell her . . ." The rest of the message was garbled. Julie couldn't hear the person over the music.

"What?" She rummaged around on Alexia's desk for a scrap of paper.

"Tell her Reggie McDonald called. Have her call me as soon as she gets in."

"Okay, what's your number?" Julie grabbed a pencil.

"It's 555-6836. Thanks. Bye."

Click. The person hung up. Julie didn't recognize the voice or the name. Reggie. What kind of a name was that? How would you spell it?

Julie wrote an R on a pink Post-it. Was it R-E-J or R-G? And was it an E or an I at the end? Finally she wrote: "RGE Caled."

Now what was the number again? It was 555 . . . something. She wrote 555 down. The second part had a 6, a 3, and an 8. She wrote the three numbers down and tossed the paper and pencil back on Alexia's desk. Then she headed downstairs to put the phone back in the kitchen where it belonged.

"Julie?"

"I'll be right up, Bean. I'll bring a snack."

Julie took the last two graham crackers and poured orange juice into two plastic glasses. She was headed back upstairs when the front door swung open, startling her so that she nearly spilled the orange juice. Alexia strode in, leaving the door open behind her. In a single motion, she dropped her backpack and jacket in a chair and kept walking straight through to the kitchen. "Hey, babe," she called to Julie, giving her a nod. Then she added in an annoying singsong voice, "Not supposed to eat in the living room."

Julie looked at the glasses and crackers balanced in her hands. She kicked the front door closed and followed her bossy sister back into the kitchen. "I was just going upstairs. And don't call me babe." That was another thing Alexia had started doing when she began high school. She even called Mom and Dad babe sometimes. Julie thought it sounded stupid. Mom and Dad said it was disrespectful.

"Any phone calls?" Alexia stuck her arm into the cookie jar.

"There's a message on your desk," Julie told her.

Alexia's hand came up empty. "Who ate all the cookies?"

"You did," Julie said.

Julie studied her sister as she searched in the refrigerator for something to eat. Alexia had cut her brown hair short and dyed it black. Mom had had a fit. Alexia said it was to show off her earrings. She had five holes in her left ear, with tiny silver earrings all the way around her earlobe. Julie thought it was neat, but she couldn't stand the thought of Alexia's girlfriend making those holes with a needle and a potato.

Alexia slammed the refrigerator door. "There's never anything good to eat around here since Mom started working." She grabbed the phone and headed up the stairs. "Who called?"

"I don't know."

Julie followed Alexia, still balancing the snacks for herself and Bean.

"Where's the message?" Alexia yelled from her room. Loud music was already blasting from her CD player.

"On your desk." Julie stood in the doorway and motioned with her elbow. "The pink paper."

Alexia went to her desk and frantically pushed paper around. "Where? This?" She held the pink scrap in her hand. "I can't read this." Her voice rose. "What the heck does it say?" She stuck the paper in Julie's face.

Julie couldn't read it either. She looked at the R. "Rrrr," she tried to sound it out. "Rrr. Ga."

"Julie!" Alexia said in an exasperated voice. "Was it a guy or a girl?"

"I'm not sure. It sounded like a guy." How was

she supposed to know? Alexia had a million kids calling all the time. The phone was always ringing for her. None of Julie's friends could ever get through, for crying out loud.

Alexia groaned like someone had hit her.

"I got the number anyway," Julie told her.

"What is it?" Jeez! Alexia sounded like this was a matter of life or death or something.

Julie looked at the paper. "It's 555-638."

Alexia waited. She stared at Julie like she had two heads. "Is that it? Six numbers?"

Julie nodded. "Look, I couldn't hear good, okay? The dumb music was playing."

"I don't believe it. You are *so* stupid!" Alexia screamed. "You can't even take a phone message. You shouldn't be allowed to answer the phone." She turned abruptly back into her room and slammed the door.

"You're the stupid one," Julie called through the door, but she knew her sister couldn't hear her over the music. She was probably already on the phone, trying to find out who the R person was. Julie glared at the door with the Mad Hatter poster on it. Suddenly her eyes were blurry with tears. She wished Dad would get home right now. He was supposed to be back before 6:00. She could see out the hall window that the clear blue March sky was being swallowed up by dark. What if something bad had happened? What if his heart stopped and Dad never came home?

Three

JULIE'S BACKPACK FELT even heavier than usual when she came down for breakfast on Wednesday. Both Dad and Mom had gotten home late the night before. Then everything had gone wrong. Alexia had forgotten to put the casserole in the oven. Dinner was late and Bean was whiny and Dad got angry because Mom reminded him he was supposed to be losing weight to help his heart. Julie knew her "poor work" papers would just make everything worse, so they never got signed, and now they were scrunched up in the bottom of her pack. She would show them to her parents tonight. Old

Spit would just have to wait another day.

Mom was racing around the kitchen trying to get Bean his cereal. Julie still couldn't get used to seeing her mother dressed for work. Today she had on a navy-blue suit and red high heels. Her dark hair hung in curls at her shoulders. She was pretty, Julie thought, but she always seemed tired or upset or busy.

"No milk," Mom groaned instead of saying good morning. "Julie, can you make up some powdered milk? I'll be late for work."

"Sure," Julie said, even though she hated powdered milk.

"Thanks. Dad will be down in a minute. Have a good day, guys." Mom squeezed Julie and kissed Bean on the top of the head. Then she was gone.

Bean pounded his fist on the table. "I hate powdered milk."

"No problem," Julie told him. "We'll have cinnamon toast instead."

"Yummmm." Bean gave her the thumbs-up sign, and Julie poured Bean's bowl of Toasty Os, the cheap brand of Cheerios, back in the box.

As she popped the bread into the toaster, Julie remembered today was Scholars Day, the day all the smart kids in her class got to go to Greenville School and do neat stuff.

Julie hated Scholars Day. She walked slowly down the steep hill to school, passing the tiny colorful houses perched like steps on the hillside. Sometimes she pretended a giant could climb the mountain on those steps. Today she just dragged one foot after the other, thinking about how she and Sara James were the only girls left behind with the dumb kids on Scholars Day.

Glenda, Abby, and Ruth Ann were all standing by the fourth- and fifth-grade entrance when Julie arrived.

"Hey, Julie," Glenda called. "You're invited, too." She stuck a small envelope into Julie's hand.

"Glenda's having a birthday party," Abby explained. Her curly black hair was unbrushed, as usual. Abby didn't care about stuff like hairstyles; that was one reason she was Julie's best friend. They had been in the same class every year since kindergarten.

"Yeah, my mom says no boys allowed and I have to invite the Brain." Glenda rolled her eyes and pushed her short blond hair behind her ears. "Just because her mother and my mom are friends." She made her voice higher and rocked her head back and forth. "Marlene could read when she was four years old. She skipped second grade. She is a *brilliant* flutist." The other girls giggled. Julie glanced over at Marlene, who was already at the curb waiting for the bus. She was sure glad her mother wasn't friends with Glenda's mom. What was so bad about reading when you were four, anyway? She bet Bean could learn.

The bell rang. Glenda, Ruth Ann, and Abby headed for the bus to Greenville School. Abby was the only one who said good-bye. "See you this afternoon," she called over her shoulder. "Write me a note."

"Sure," Julie mumbled. She hated Wednesdays. Those kids would all come back talking about the neat things they were doing at Greenville, like extra science projects and writing real books that you could send away and get printed. So what? Julie thought. She hated science and reading anyway.

As she walked to her classroom, she opened the envelope Glenda had given her. There was a butterfly sticker on the back. The card had a rainbow and flowers on the front. It said, "You are invited." Julie skipped over the little poem on the inside. She read

"Come to my . . ." The next word started with an S. It was long and it was in cursive. Julie guessed at the word without sounding it out. "Sleepover." She stuck the card and envelope in her pocket. Of course Glenda's mom wouldn't let boys come. Leave it to Glenda to even think about having boys to a sleep-over. She peeled off her coat. She was glad she was invited to the party, even if Glenda was kind of a show-off. But now she had to face a day with Mrs. Spattelli and none of her friends.

Brian got picked to pass back the math tests. "Nobody in this classroom today did well on this test, so we are going to go over each problem together." What Mrs. Spattelli meant was that none of the stupid kids in this classroom could do math. Julie felt tired already. Even her pencil seemed heavy.

As Brian came to her desk, she sat up straighter. She could tell the next paper was hers. It was marked F, with a line to be signed. Another "poor work" paper to bring home! Brian laid it on her desk and made a face. Julie slapped her hand over the grade, avoiding Brian's eyes.

"All right," the teacher was saying. "We'll start

with number one. Sara, you read the problem."

Sara sniffed and wiped her nose with a tissue from the little box she kept on her desk. Half the time she was absent because of her allergies. So what? Julie hardly ever hung out with Sara anyway. "Reduce three twenty-fourths to the lowest terms," Mrs. Spit commanded in a raspy voice. Julie wished she could be absent. She wanted to go to the nurse and tell her she was allergic to school.

Sara didn't know the answer. Julie looked at the numbers. Glenda's party was on 3/24. She could make a card for Glenda. She'd use her colored pencils if Bean hadn't ruined all of them. Maybe she could make something for March. Flowers, tulips.

"Julie, are you going to join the class?" Mrs. Spattelli was staring at her. So were all fourteen of the dumb kids left in this dumb class. Brian snickered behind her.

Julie felt her face get hot. "Yes," she stammered.

"Well, then you should know we are on number four."

The day dragged on. It was practically all workbook stuff and review. It always was on Wednesday. Boring. At least last year Julie used to get to go to Mrs. Stuart, the reading teacher, on Wednesday. But Mrs. Stuart only worked with kids up to third grade. Mrs. Stuart was fun. She played games and sometimes they just talked.

Brian got kept in at lunch recess for making noise in the halls. So Julie didn't even have a chance to win back her shooter. After lunch she sat on the blacktop with her back against the brick wall of the school. Sara was playing with some third-grade kids whom Julie didn't know. Sometimes Julie played with the kindergartners on Wednesday, but it was late and recess for the little kids was just ending.

Julie watched the first graders and kindergartners line up. Then she took her sack of marbles out of her jacket pocket, walked over to the edge of the blacktop and made a circle on the dirt. Dad had given her the marbles for her birthday. He said he used to play marbles all the time when he was a kid. Julie thought it was neat. The marbles came with a book about how to play. It had lots of pictures in it. She started bringing the book and marbles to school, and now some of the other kids, mostly boys, were bringing marbles, too. Julie taught them how to play.

Glenda said nobody played marbles anymore, but Julie didn't care. She lined up the glass balls and shot them into the circle. One by one, she got them all in. Julie sighed and picked up the marbles. She could have beaten Brian and Nate yesterday. Today recess was too long. Julie looked up and saw Sara standing at the edge of the blacktop.

"What are you looking at?" Julie snapped.

Sara didn't answer. Julie took the marble out of the circle and began shooting again.

"Glenda says marbles are for babies," Sara said.

"So what?" Julie glanced up at Sara.

Sara sniffed. "So does Abby."

Julie stood up. "How do you know?"

The bell rang and Sara turned around and headed toward the door. Julie scooped up her marbles. Who cared what Sara said?

After lunch they had social studies and science, more workbook stuff. Finally it was time for free reading. They always had free reading on Wednesday afternoons because all the brains got back right in the middle of last period, and Mrs. Spit said it was impossible to teach anything with the interruption. Mrs. Spit didn't like anything except regular down-to-business schoolwork.

Julie took her favorite book out of her desk cubby—*Clara Saves the Day*. She liked adventure stories, preferably short books with words she knew. *Clara Saves the Day* had only a few hard words and was just 48 pages long. Julie had already read it once at home. Now she was reading it for a book report. Stories about pioneers and Indians were her favorite. This was a pioneer story. Julie didn't know if Mrs. Spit would accept it for a fourth-grade report because it was too short. Julie didn't care; she was reading it anyway. Mrs. Stuart said it was the reading, not the length that counted. Julie was just at the part where Clara had to go alone at night to the next settlement for help when the smart kids got back. They were all talking out in the hall, slamming their lockers.

Mrs. Spattelli jumped up from her desk and opened the classroom door to shush them. Quickly Julie closed her book and slipped it into her desk cubby under the pile of workbooks. She pulled out a library copy of *Maniac Magee*. It was hardcover, with real chapters, and it was 184 pages long. Julie had had the book for a week, and she was still on the first page.

Abby passed Julie's desk and tapped the cover of *Maniac*. "Great book," she whispered, smiling. "I read it in two days."

Julie knew that this was Abby's favorite book. She made a little wave and smiled back. "Yeah," she whispered.

"Where's my note?" Abby asked.

Julie glanced over her shoulder. Mrs. Spit was still herding kids through the door. "I forgot."

"I wrote you one. It's in my backpack." Abby bent over and looked at the page Julie was opened to. "What part are you on?" She reached out to open the book wider.

Julie slapped the covers together. "Never mind," she hissed. "It's none of your business."

"Sor-*ry!*" Abby spoke out loud, stressing the last syllable. She turned her back to Julie, stomped across the room, and slumped huffily into her seat.

"Girls!"

Julie felt Mrs. Spattelli's hard look but she kept her eyes down. Abby had done an oral book report on *Maniac* at the beginning of the year. She made it sound great.

Julie took a deep breath and opened the book again. Hunching over it so no one could see what page she was on, Julie read the first paragraph over for the hundredth time. She didn't see what was so great about it. She had to keep sounding out words and then going to the beginning again. It didn't make any sense. She stared at the page, but the longer she looked, the more jumbled the letters all got. Julie hated reading. What was she going to do when it was her turn to give an oral book report and Abby and Glenda found out she could only read baby books? The tips of her ears burned at the thought. Why couldn't she be good at something?

Four

"*PREHENSILE!* I KNOW what that is," Bean sang out at the dinner table. "It's when you have a thumb like peoples and monkeys. You can do this." He held up a butter knife between his flat palm and his thumb.

Clank. The knife fell, hitting a plate and bouncing to the floor.

Dad made a face and leaned over to pick up the knife. "Hey, Bean, that's great. Where did you learn that?"

"Probably from the TV," Alexia said sarcastically.

"That's all that kid does." She was slumped over her plate, both elbows on the table.

"I did not, I learned it from Julie. She told me that's one thing that makes us whuman beans."

"And you're one smart whuman, Bean." Dad laughed and reached out to ruffle Bean's hair. He smiled at Julie. "And you've got one smart sister. You're lucky to have her."

"By the way, smartie," Alexia scoffed, "Reggie is short for Regina and she's a girl. Just for the record, she knows I have an idiot for a sister."

"Don't take it out on me just because it's your dish night."

"Just because you can't even answer the *phone,*" Alexia shot back.

"Girls." Dad frowned at both of them. "That's enough." He turned to Bean. "Your teacher told me today that you are the only one in your class who knows your whole address and telephone number. Put her there, guy," said Dad, giving Bean the high sign. Bean slapped him five and giggled.

"Julie taught me."

Alexia screwed up her face and mimicked, "Julie taught me," without making a sound.

Julie caught her sister's antics out of the corner of her eye. Lucky for Alexia Mom wasn't there. She wouldn't let her get away with that stuff.

When Mom worked late, Dad made dinner. Dad didn't care if you ate your veggies, and he always made great stuff like hamburgers and French fries. Tonight they were having macaroni and cheese out of the box—Julie's favorite. She liked to see if she could slip one macaroni over each prong of the fork without using her fingers. She did it!

"Look," she said, holding up her fork with four yellow noodles sticking up like fingers.

"Hey, neat." Bean picked up a noodle to put on his fork. It squished between his fingers.

"Not like that, Bean." Julie laughed and sucked the noodles off her fork with a loud slurp.

"You two are disgusting!" Alexia pushed her chair back and stood up in one motion. "Can't we ever have a decent meal around here?" She picked up her plate and headed out of the dining room toward the kitchen. "And everyone wonders why I don't invite my friends over. Jeez!"

Dad shrugged his shoulders and winked. "Hormones," he whispered.

"What's hormones?" Bean asked.

"Chemicals that turn teenagers into monsters." Dad put his hands over his head like monster claws.

Julie giggled. She leaned over, hugged Dad, and gave him a loud kiss on the cheek.

"What did I do to deserve a cheddar cheese kiss?" Dad made a big deal of wiping his cheek, then looking at his outstretched hand. "Hmmm, a whole dinner right there on this palm." He pretended he was going to lick it.

"You're gross," Julie told him.

Dad leaned back in his chair and stretched. He brought his hands down over his belly. "What did you kids make me eat all that macaroni and cheese for, anyway?" He stood up. "Come on, Beano. Let's get you down."

Bean stood up in his booster seat with outstretched arms. Dad grabbed him by the wrists and swung him down to the floor. "Pleeease, Daddy, let's do airplane." Bean reached up again.

Dad frowned. "Can't do that, Beano," he said.

"Come on, Bean, you leave Dad alone now. I'll give you a piggyback ride," Julie said quickly. She squatted down so Bean could climb on her back. "Once around the living room. Then I have homework."

"Giddap, Julie."

* * *

Upstairs at her desk, Julie pulled her homework papers out of her backpack. They were all crumpled up with the "poor work" papers. There were the two from yesterday and today's F from math. Mrs. Spattelli had forgotten to ask for them. She wished she could throw them all into the trash, even the homework. Instead she pressed each one out with her hands and made two piles, one for homework and the other for papers Mom and Dad had to see.

Then she picked up her math book and opened it to page 68. The first five problems were easy. But as Julie was writing number six on the paper, she remembered that they were supposed to do only the even numbers. She flipped her pencil around and started to erase the answers to numbers one, three, and five. Now her paper was a mess. Julie brushed the bits of eraser away and erased some more. The metal rim of the pencil caught the paper and tore it. Julie flattened out the torn piece with her fingernail. Now Mrs. Spattelli would really yell at her for sloppy work.

Julie flipped through her book. She had one piece of plain, clean, unlined paper left. It was newsprint Mrs. Spit had passed out for the math homework.

The pages of the math book fell open right at the place Julie had stuck her paper. It was there with the invitation to Glenda's party. Julie studied the design with the flowers and the rainbow and the butterfly sticker. Suddenly she had a great idea for a March birthday card. She pushed her homework aside, took the clean sheet out of the book and creased it twice so it folded like a card.

Today on the way home from school Julie had seen some little kid and his mom with a kite out in the graveyard at the top of their street. It was perfect kite weather. A kite would be the perfect decoration for a March birthday card. She pulled open the bottom desk drawer and took out a piece of origami paper she had been saving for something special. It was her favorite, her last piece, the only one in the package that had designs on it. There were flowers in pink, white, orange, and gold. Julie folded the paper into a diamond kite shape and glued it onto the card. Next she got a piece of yarn from her weaving kit and tied little pieces of blue, yellow, and green crepe paper along it. She stuck the yarn on the bottom of the kite so it hung down like the tail of a real kite.

She glued some bits of doily on the bottom of the

card for flowers, then she colored the doilies with marker. The card looked great. It was one of the best things she had ever made. Maybe she shouldn't give it to Glenda, Julie thought. Maybe she should keep it. She piled her art supplies neatly on one corner of her desk with the card. She still had to do the inside. She didn't want to rush. Mom kept some shiny ribbon for special gifts and crafts. Julie needed some for the card, but she had to ask Mom where it was. She could always finish later and decide if she would give it to Glenda.

"Bedtime for Bean." Dad was coming up the stairs. Julie could tell from the footsteps that Bean was with him. She looked at the clock. It was already past Bean's bedtime. Dad always forgot about bedtime when Mom wasn't home. She had missed all her TV time. Julie couldn't believe it. Who cared—the card was more fun anyway.

Julie admired it again, then rushed to the bedroom door. "Look what I made."

Dad studied the card. "Hey, this is great, freckle face. You are one talented kid. Sure don't know where you get it from. I can't even draw a straight line."

Julie giggled.

“That reminds me, we need to get Beano a kite,” Dad said.

Julie nodded.

“When?” Bean piped in.

“Soon,” Dad said, “but not before you two get a good night’s sleep. Homework all done, Julie? You two had better get to bed before your mother gets in. She’ll have my hide.”

“Yep.” The answer was out before she even thought. Julie glanced at her desk with the math homework and the “poor work” papers all pushed aside. Her good mood was spoiled. Quickly, before Dad could ask any questions, Julie stuffed the papers back into her pack. She tried to stuff her frustration about homework and lying in with them.

Julie was already in bed with the lights out when she heard Mom tiptoe into the room and whisper, “Good night.” She pretended to be asleep. Mom pulled the covers up and kissed her. The faint smell of the perfume that her mother wore to work reminded Julie about all the changes in their house lately. It made her feel worse than ever.

Five

MOM SAID SHE wouldn't have time to take Julie shopping. They decided she would just pick up a gift on the way home from work one day before the party. Julie told her to get anything, whatever was easy, but not a book like Mom had suggested—maybe one of those little backpack purses. Mom loved the card. She said Julie should give it to Glenda, since she wasn't picking out the gift. It was more personal.

"I'm sure Glenda and the other girls will appreciate your handiwork and that's what you made it for." Mom was in a good mood. "I'll try to get some more origami paper if you want to make another one to keep."

"Hey, Glenda," Julie called to her classmate as she entered the school playground. "My mom wants to know what time she should pick me up from the party."

Glenda was with the usual gang—Abby, Ruth Ann, and Sara. "My mother says she wants everyone out by nine," she said loudly, glancing over to where Marlene stood by herself. Julie thought Marlene was like a satellite, always hovering around the other girls but never really doing anything with them. On the other hand, Glenda was like the sun, with everyone always crowded around her like the planets. She always had to be the center of attention. Now Glenda bent her head down and whispered, "But you guys can stay until ten. At least we'll have an hour without the Brain." Ruth Ann giggled.

Julie glanced back at Marlene. She was acting like she hadn't heard, but her ears were red. Julie edged over toward Abby. "Want to see if we can go to the party together? I bet my mom or dad could drive."

Abby turned her back. Without saying a word, she walked around to the other side of the group and started talking to Ruth Ann. Julie didn't know what to do. She felt like Abby had hit her. Her cheeks burned. Slowly it dawned on her that Abby was still mad about yesterday. She cringed as the words "none of your business" came back to her.

Julie turned quickly and walked to the steps at the front entrance like nothing had happened. She sat down and opened her backpack. Without even taking out the notebook, she tore out a piece of lined paper. With a pink marker from the pocket in her pack, she wrote "SORRY, I SAW A JERK" in big letters. She sketched a quick silly picture of herself with her tongue hanging out and her eyes crossed. Then she drew three flowers and a happy face. "Love, Julie." As she read the note over, she groaned. Shaking her head, she put a big X through *saw* and wrote *was*. Quickly, before she could find any more mistakes, Julie folded the note six times until it was real small. Abby liked to get notes. Maybe this would get her to make up. Julie really wanted to tell her friend that Glenda was being a jerk about Marlene and her party. But she thought she'd better wait until they were speaking again.

The bell rang and Julie walked by herself to the fourth-grade classroom. She stopped short just inside the door. Someone in a blue dress with curly black hair was writing on the board, and it sure wasn't Mrs. Spattelli. The other kids started piling into the room. Nate bumped right into Julie. "Hey, get outta—" He stopped dead in his tracks. "We got a sub," he said out loud. Then he whispered, "Man, Brian! We got a sub." They slapped each other five. Julie couldn't believe it. Any minute now something would break the spell and that new person in the front of the room would turn back into Mrs. Spit. Julie would be doomed to another day without lunch recess, sitting in a hot room after eating, doing makeup work instead of getting to go outside.

The person at the blackboard had turned around. She still hadn't changed back into their regular teacher, and she was pretty. Julie started to feel good. Now she didn't have to worry about the math homework she hadn't done or the papers she didn't have signed. Now she had another chance to finish the homework and get all the papers signed tonight.

Julie waited by the door until Abby took her seat. Then she walked past, tossed the folded note onto her friend's desk, and kept walking to her seat. When she went by Brian, he made an *ooo* noise. "No note-passing," he whispered.

Julie looked back and mouthed the words "shut up." Before she turned to take her seat, Abby waved and smiled. Julie waved back. Brian was a pain, but who cared? Her best friend wasn't mad at her anymore. This was going to be a great day.

Finally everyone was seated, waiting to find out who the new teacher was.

"My name is Ms. Eddie. I will be your substitute for today."

Brian and Nate cheered. So did a few other kids.

"That will be enough." Ms. Eddie began taking attendance. Then she collected lunch money just the way Mrs. Spattelli did, only the class was noisy. Glenda kept getting out of her seat to help Ms. Eddie find things. Ms. Eddie asked her to sit down twice, but when it was time to take the attendance sheet and money envelope to the office, Glenda was right up there at the teacher's desk again. Julie glanced over at Abby, who made a face. They both laughed.

Behind her, Brian kept slapping his ruler on the desk and tapping the eraser end of a pencil. Slap. Tap-tap, tap-tap. He was humming, too. A real one-man band, Julie thought. He wouldn't get away with it if Mrs. Spit were here. All during math, she felt like turning around and smacking Brian with his own ruler.

"Okay, class, you can put your work away. Mrs. Spattelli says you are going to have a unit test when she gets back, so let's practice with a spelling bee."

Great. Julie hated spelling bees. She always went out on her first word. Then she had to sit and watch all her friends go on and on spelling perfectly.

Of course Glenda had to tell Ms. Eddie exactly how they lined up on either side of the room when Mrs. Spattelli was there. "I can tell you who the best spellers are so the poor spellers don't all get on the same team," Glenda added.

Why didn't Ms. Eddie tell Glenda to keep quiet? This day was not as fun as Julie thought it would be.

Everyone lined up, left side or right side, as the sub called their names. That put Julie third in line on the right side of the room. She tried to inch her way toward the end so at least she wouldn't be the first person to sit down. She had moved down only two places when Ms. Eddie clapped her hands. Julie squeezed in between Darlene Flanagan and Jason Elliott. "Please stand tall and quiet, right where you are." She stressed the last four words. Julie could feel her glare.

Being midway down the line didn't do any good.

Everyone ahead of her got the easy words. Even Brian got the word *homesick*—two easy words stuck together.

Julie wet her lips as Sara spelled *babble.* It was her turn next.

"*Trouble.*" Ms. Eddie said the word. "I do not want to have to report any trouble to Mrs. Spattelli. Trouble."

Julie took a deep breath. "Trouble." She sounded it out in her head. Trubull. "T-r-u-b-u-l-l."

"Buzzzzz." Nate made the sound of a game-show buzzer. "Wrong," he said in a nasal voice. Everyone laughed.

Julie could feel her face heating up. She walked quickly back to her seat, but it seemed to take forever. For the first time ever, she missed Mrs. Spattelli. No one would have gotten away with that kind of behavior if she were here. She sat down, crossed her arms on her desk, and buried her head in them. Maybe she could hide that way until her face cooled off.

"Those who sit down need to listen," Ms. Eddie said. Julie was the only one sitting down and she knew Ms. Eddie really meant "the dumb ones like you, Julie, need to listen." Julie raised her head and leaned her chin on her fist with her elbow on the desk, like she was bored. Like she didn't care in the least about stupid spelling words or stupid Ms. Eddie or the rest of this stupid class.

Six

MORE AND MORE kids started missing their words and had to sit down. Sara missed *helicopter* and Brian missed *mechanic.* He crossed his eyes at Julie when he passed her desk. Julie let out a deep sigh. Sara was sniffing and trying to clean her nose with a used tissue. Gross. Julie looked away.

"Those of you who are sitting in your seats, please be polite," Ms. Eddie said for the third time. Everyone sitting out kept whispering and talking.

Didn't she know how dumb she sounded? At least when Mrs. Spattelli said to be quiet, kids listened. Julie rested her head on her arms on the desktop again. Then she remembered the teacher had already yelled at her for that, so she sat up and tried to pay attention. But she couldn't concentrate with all the mumbling and whispering, and with Brian doing his one-man band routine again. The next word was *parachute*. Nate shouted the letters out over the noise from the class.

"That does it!" Ms. Eddie's face was red. "People sitting down, take out your spelling books and a piece of notebook paper. Write each word in the chapter 8 review section ten times. If you don't finish, you will do it for homework."

It wasn't fair. Julie wasn't even talking. Fifty words, ten times each. It would take forever. Julie shoved her hand in her cubby and grabbed her spelling book and a piece of paper. She slammed the book down on the desk and slapped her pencil down next to it. She flipped to page 149 and began to write the word *butter.* Ten times!

Julie barely listened to the spellers. Four people were left. Everyone else was rustling papers and pages.

"*Molecule,*" Ms. Eddie said.

It was Glenda's word. Of course she got it right. The word *molecule* made Julie think of the Captain Science show she saw about how molecules are always bumping into each other. Julie wished she could see the molecules floating around, bouncing off each other. She imagined them to be all colors, like tiny round marbles, tapping into each other and shooting off in opposite directions.

Marbles! Yesterday she'd left them hidden in her desk. She hadn't meant to. Things were always disappearing out of desks. Kids took pencils and erasers, especially when they changed seats for reading groups and stuff. She hadn't seen them this morning. Suddenly she had to know for sure if her marbles were missing. She couldn't wait. With her right hand, Julie continued to write her spelling words. Slowly she inched her left hand inside the cubby under her desk.

The marbles were supposed to be on the left, under her social studies book. Her cubby was a mess. The book was buried under papers and workbooks and a box of crayons.

The whole class had finally quieted down now. Julie did not want to attract attention. Her fingers brushed the soft fabric of the bag. There they were. Slowly she inched the marble pouch toward her out from under the pile of books. She held her breath, staring at her spelling book, pretending to write the words on her paper. Marlene was spelling *arithmetic* as Julie slid the marbles toward her. She wanted to make sure the drawstring was pulled tight.

"Hey, Julie." Thwack! Brian's ruler came down on her shoulder.

"Ouch!" Julie jerked forward and reached back for the ruler. Her pencil flew out of her hand and her spelling paper floated to the floor. At the same time she bumped her left hand on the side of her cubby, knocking the whole pouch of glass balls onto the floor. Julie held her breath as every one of her twenty-seven marbles and three shooters bounced and rolled and slid in all directions across the smooth linoleum. The crash seemed to last forever.

For an instant the room was silent. Julie's face felt like it was going to burn up. Then everyone started talking at once, drowning out Marlene's winning spelling performance.

"Here, Julie." Several kids handed her marbles.

"I got one," Nate yelled from across the room.

Julie scurried on the floor, desperate to scoop up the rest. All she wanted to do was stuff her pouch back in the desk and pretend nothing had happened. Marlene had won the spelling bee and now they could go to lunch.

"Julie." She didn't dare look up, but the tips of Ms. Eddie's brown shoes with the chunky heels were in front of her nose. "Are those your marbles?"

Julie nodded as she reached out to retrieve her orange and white shooter from under Brian's desk.

"Pick them up and bring them to me." She turned around and went back to the front of the classroom. "Everyone else, in your seats and be quiet." Julie could feel the whole class staring at her. She concentrated on stuffing marbles in her pouch. When the last one was in, she yanked the drawstrings and brought the marbles to Ms. Eddie, hoping none were missing.

The whole class watched as the sub held out her hand. Julie dropped the pouch into it, turned abruptly, and hurried back to her seat. She sat down just in time to see the teacher put the pouch into the top drawer on the right-hand side of Mrs. Spattelli's desk. "Julie, I want you to write a report on 'Why I Should Not Play with Marbles in School.' It should fill two sides of one piece of notebook paper. You will have your parents sign it and bring it in to Mrs. Spattelli tomorrow, if I'm not here. I'm leaving a note for her."

Brian let out a soft whistle.

Julie knew her face was the color of Sara's red blouse. "But"—her voice came out in a croak—"I wasn't playing."

"That will be enough, Julie. You can have your marbles back after school. Class, get ready for lunch."

Everyone got up and headed for the coat closet like nothing had happened. Julie grabbed her lunch bag and got in line. She kept her eyes on the floor. A stupid report on top of writing spelling words ten times each. It was going to take all night for nothing. It wasn't fair. She hadn't been talking and she hadn't been playing with marbles. Ms. Eddie was worse than Mrs. Spattelli. This was a rotten day.

Out on the playground Julie watched Nate and Brian shoot marbles. Brian still had her special shooter, the one that was blue and green like a globe.

"Julie, what's the matter? Lost your marbles?" Nate called.

"I get it. Lost your marbles." Brian laughed. "Lost your marbles." He slapped his leg and acted like it was the funniest thing anyone ever said. "Maybe Ms. Eddie can win back your shooter." He held up the large blue and green glass marble just to rub it in.

"What's so funny, Brian? It was your fault, jerk."

"Was not."

"Next time you hit me with that stupid ruler I'm going to break it." Julie kicked a pebble into the game and walked away.

"Jeez, I was just going to ask what word you were on." She heard Brian trying to explain, but she kept on walking. Tears sprang to her eyes. All she wanted to do was go away by herself, but Abby was coming across the playground.

"Hi." Julie tried to smile. At least her friend wasn't still mad.

"Hey," Abby said. "Thanks for the note." She hesitated and then said, "Sorry about your marbles."

"It's okay." Julie didn't want to talk about it, even with Abby. "Hey, what are you getting Glenda?"

"I got a stuffed animal. It's a baby zebra. It's *soooo* cute. I can't wait till she sees it. What are you getting?"

"I told my mom to get one of those denim purses like Alexia has. But I'm making a real neat card."

"Shhh, here she comes."

"Isn't the sub *soooo* nice?" Glenda greeted them. Ruth Ann and Sara were with her.

As usual Marlene was a few feet away, looking

like she didn't even know what to do with her hands. Annoying, Julie thought.

Suddenly a cheer went up from the boys at the marble game. Brian was jumping around like a lunatic.

The girls turned toward them. "I think the sub is mean," Abby said. "She took Julie's marbles."

Glenda shrugged and turned away from the boys. "Who cares about marbles? It's a dumb game. Wait until you see what games we're going to play at my party." The girls moved to the steps where they usually sat and talked at recess. Of course Glenda sat in the middle. She always had to be in the middle of everything!

Julie stayed on the blacktop instead of following the other girls. She was tired of hearing about Glenda's party. If she had her marbles, she'd be winning her shooter back from Brian and probably taking a few of his, too. As soon as the dismissal bell rang, she was going to ask Ms. Eddie for her marbles. She was going to get them back and tell the sub what really happened. She hadn't been playing. And none of this would have happened if Brian hadn't hit her shoulder with his dumb ruler.

Julie watched the clock all afternoon. At two it was time for gym. Ms. Eddie made them line up in alphabetical order. It took forever.

"Mr. Latrobe is sure going to be mad when we're late for gym," Glenda said.

Ms. Eddie must have been getting tired of Glenda, because she just told her to find her place in line. Glenda crossed her arms over her chest and pouted.

"Are you gonna tell your mommy?" Brian asked Glenda in a baby voice.

Ms. Eddie glared at him. By the time everyone quieted down they were almost ten minutes late for gym class.

"Let's not waste any more time," Mr. Latrobe said in his big bear voice. "We are going to finish our fitness tests today so that next week we can start baseball outside." Everyone cheered. Julie didn't care much about baseball, but she liked gym and she liked being out of Mrs. Spit's room and she liked Mr. Latrobe. Today they were doing the poles.

Finally it was Julie's turn to climb. The poles folded down out of the high gym ceiling and you got to climb them and then come down like a fireman.

Back when he was a firefighter, Dad had tried it a

few times before they had remodeled the fire station and taken the pole out. He said it was neat. Only the fourth and fifth graders got to climb the poles, and Julie had been waiting since kindergarten to touch the huge gymnasium ceiling. She pulled herself up hand over hand, forgetting about everything else. Her whole body ached, but she knew she could do it. She inched upward, pulling with her arms and pushing with her feet. Every inch took her closer to the top. "Atta girl, Julie." Only about half the class had made it all the way to the ceiling.

She tagged the ceiling and grinned down at her teacher. He had a shiny bald spot on the top of his head. "Come on down." But Mr. Latrobe didn't have to tell her. Julie was already moving down that pole just like a firefighter. Just like Dad. It wasn't as easy as it looked to come down. She had to be careful not to burn her hands. But it was fun and Julie hoped she could climb the pole again sometime.

The bell rang just as she touched the floor. Julie couldn't believe it. School was over. Poor Mr. Latrobe. He still hadn't finished the fitness testing because of that dumb sub. "Sorry, kids," Mr. Latrobe said. "Time's up, and bus people are already late. Line up and get moving."

"I'll miss my bus," Glenda wailed as she pushed into line in front of Julie.

"No need to panic. No one's bus will leave without them."

At least Julie didn't have to worry about catching her bus. She could just get her stuff and go home.

When they got back to the classroom, Ms. Eddie already had her coat on. She was standing out in the hallway. "I have bus duty today. Everyone hurry up and get your coats. Walkers, you may be dismissed."

"Yessss! We're outta here." Brian stuck two thumbs up and then slapped Nate's upturned palms.

"Bus people, follow me," said Ms. Eddie and then headed down the hall.

Abby ran by Julie, her backpack hanging off her arm and her jacket dragging on the floor. "Bye." She fluttered her fingers over her shoulder on her way down the hall with the other bus kids.

Julie hoisted her backpack up over her shoulders and slowly followed the other walkers out the door. Halfway up the hill to her house she remembered her marbles. Darn! Now she would have to get them from Mrs. Spit or whoever was there tomorrow. She should never have brought them to school in the first place.

Seven

"JULIE'S HOME," BEAN'S voice rang out as the front door swung open. Julie couldn't even get her backpack off before Bean was jumping up and down in front of her waving a long, thin package. "Dad got a kite. Help me do it, Julie."

"Hey, great," Julie said. "Just give me a minute." She walked through the living room. "Dad?"

"In here, Julie." His voice came from the dining room, where he had made an office space for the new computer they got after he had had to stop work.

"How was school? What's the news?" Dad always had to know everything.

"Okay. No news." Julie said the same thing every day.

"Just okay?"

She stood by her dad's elbow watching the letters pop up on the screen. Julie got to go to the computer lab at school every other Tuesday. That was another class she liked. Dad let Julie use the computer to do homework. It wasn't like the ones they had in school, but she could usually figure it out. He said Spell Check was going to solve all her problems. Right!

"We had a sub," she mumbled now, happy that Dad was too busy to ask for details. Maybe later she'd tell him about forgetting her marbles and her punishment and having to write all those spelling words and how unfair it was.

"So! A break from the Wild Witch of Westminster School." He didn't even take his eyes off the screen, where letters just kept popping up as Dad's fingers clicked the keys.

Julie smiled. "Yeah. Hey, I see you got a kite."

"Listen, if you help Bean put it together, it will still be light enough to go up to the cemetery to see if we can find some wind when I'm done here. That is, if you don't have too much homework." Dad turned from the computer and looked at Julie.

"Not much." She slipped off her denim jacket and headed back toward the living room. Bean was on the floor in the middle of plastic wrap, kite sticks, string, and paper. "Bean?"

A huge sob shook her brother's tiny body as two big tears ran down his cheek. "I—I broke the k-kite. It's whipped."

"Oh, Bean." Julie squeezed him in a big hug. "Stop crying. It's okay."

Julie examined the torn kite paper. Dad had gotten a regular kite, the inexpensive diamond-shaped kind Julie liked best. This one was yellow with a rocket on the front. Julie rubbed Bean's back. "We can fix this even better than it was."

"You mean it?"

"Sure, we can put a patch over the rip and you can draw anything you want on it."

Bean wiped the tears off his cheeks. His eyes widened. "Can I draw an airplane?"

"Sure. Let's get to work." Julie barely got the words out when the phone rang.

She jumped up and got it on the second ring.

It was Dana, Alexia's best friend. "Hey, Julie, is Alexia there?"

"Not home yet."

"Listen, have her call as soon as she gets home. It's real important."

"Okay," Julie said.

"Thanks." Julie hung up. As she went to look for paper she remembered the last time she left a note. After the awful day she'd had, she didn't want Alexia to yell and scream again about how she couldn't read Julie's messages. It was only Dana. Julie could explain the call as soon as Alexia got home. She grabbed the message pad anyway. The paper was strong enough and just the right size for a kite patch.

Julie looked at the directions for putting the kite together, just the pictures. She always ignored the words. Bean drew an airplane on the patch paper and Julie wrote a message underneath: BEAN TAKES OF. "Bean takes off," she read to her brother.

Bean nodded seriously, and then he leaned over and squeezed Julie in a hug, practically choking her. "You're smart, Julie."

Julie giggled and pried herself free. "Thanks, Bean." She held up the kite. "Let's get some rags for a tail."

By the time they started for the cemetery, it was getting cold, but the wind was still good. Bean raced ahead with the kite. Julie ran after him, afraid he was going to break it again before it even got up in the air.

Dad seemed to be moving slowly as they headed up the hill. Julie slowed to a walk. Her own heart was beating hard and she wondered if it was okay for him to be getting so much exercise. "Let's stop here for a sec," Julie told Dad when he caught up. "I need a rest."

"I want to catch up to your brother," Dad said. "He'll about burst if we don't get this kite up."

Julie followed him, but she lagged behind, hoping maybe it would slow him down. It was Dad's heart she was worried about bursting, not the Bean.

Eight

THE WIND CAUGHT the kite and took it up as soon as Dad held it out—a yellow flash against the blue sky already beginning to get dark around the edges. He handed the string to Bean, who danced around as he held on.

Julie laughed. "Looks like that kite could carry Bean away."

Dad agreed. He liked the way she had patched the kite, too. "You sure are one clever kid," he said, hugging Julie. "But you need another F on *off*."

This was not her day. Julie sighed and Dad put his arms around her. She snuggled closer. It felt good and safe there, with Dad protecting her from the wind. They both watched Bean. He was so happy. Bean was lucky. He didn't have to go to school and have substitute teachers and worry about spelling and homework and "poor work" notices. Julie wished she could be four years old again. Even flying a kite wasn't quite so exciting anymore.

But when it was her turn to hold the kite string she forgot all about her troubles. The kite dipped and soared like it was playing a game with her. Julie wondered how far it would go if the string broke. She'd like to send all her troubles off on the wind, all fifty spelling words, ten times each, and the whole two-page report on "Why I Should Not Play with Marbles in School." The wind could carry them all away.

"Julie, don't you just wish you could fly?" Bean yelled as he ran ahead and tried to stay under the kite.

"Sure," Julie yelled. "But don't you try it!" Once she had tried to fly off the top of the couch and split her lip on the metal part of the coffee table instead.

"Not *really* fly," Bean said. "I'm not that dumb." With his arms stretched out to the sides, he zoomed down the cemetery road like it was a runway. Julie and Dad laughed. They brought the kite in, and Bean jumped up and down trying to catch the tail. Julie told Dad and Bean about climbing the pole in school and how she had touched the ceiling. Dad was impressed.

"I need help with some math homework," Julie said as they were headed home. One of the "poor work" papers was her math test from yesterday. The one with an F. Julie thought if she got one paper corrected and signed at a time, it wouldn't be so bad. Maybe if Mrs. Spattelli was really sick, she could even get them all signed before her teacher got back.

"I think we can manage that," Dad said.

Julie squeezed his hand.

"What's for dinner?" Alexia greeted them at the door.

"Cheeseburgers," Dad said cheerfully.

"Jeez, is Mom late again? We just had hamburgers two days ago."

Julie could tell from the scowl that her sister was in another one of her moods.

Alexia pulled open the refrigerator door. "Don't we

have anything else? I refuse to eat another burger."

"On what grounds," Dad asked, "religious or health?"

"Both," Alexia said. "Meat is unhealthy, and we just saw a movie in school today about what they do to those poor animals just so we can eat them. I don't think I could even watch you eat a hamburger."

"I see," said Dad. "Well, there's always peanut butter and lettuce."

"Yuck," Bean sang out.

"Dad, I'm serious." Alexia slammed the refrigerator door shut and glared at her father. "You shouldn't be eating that stuff either."

For once Julie agreed with her sister, but she didn't say anything.

"Listen, young lady," Dad said, "it's not your job to tell me what to eat. Now, it's Julie's night to set the table. When she's done, I'd like you to help her with her math homework while I make cheeseburgers. You can eat a salad and cheese, or peanut butter if you prefer."

Great! Julie would rather do her homework with a boa constrictor wrapped around her neck than have Alexia help her.

Alexia looked as if Dad had just condemned her to a year of hard labor. "But I have my own homework."

"Alexia, we all have to help out around here. Julie is setting the table. You can spend twenty minutes helping her with fourth-grade math."

"It's okay, Dad," Julie said.

Dad called after her, "It won't hurt Alexia to help out."

Alexia made a face that Dad couldn't see. "Hurry up," she snapped. "I have other stuff to do." Julie was already on her way up the stairs, but she heard her sister mumble, "Don't see why anyone needs help with fourth-grade work, anyway."

I don't need your help, Julie wanted to scream at her sister. But she was afraid Dad would hear.

Upstairs at her desk, Julie stared at the math paper. It was a unit test: multiplication problems done out across the paper, instead of up and down. She had gotten all but two wrong. How had she done so badly?

Alexia took the paper out of Julie's hand and stared at it. "You're supposed to get this signed," she said.

"Dad knows," Julie lied.

"Julie," Alexia practically screamed, "you have more than half of these right. You just put all the answers on the wrong line. God! How dumb can you get. Look." She slapped the paper down on the desk. "The teacher even made a note. Are you sure Dad saw this?"

Julie nodded. It didn't seem like lying if it was only your sister.

The phone rang and Alexia was out of the room like there was a fire.

Julie stared at her paper. She wasn't sure which was worse: to get the math wrong or to be so stupid that she put the right answers on the wrong lines. At least she could fix it without Alexia.

"Julie!" Alexia appeared in the doorway, red-faced. "When did Dana call?"

"After school," Julie murmured. "I forgot."

"But she told you it was important," Alexia screeched. She picked up a book and threw it at Julie. "I really can't stand you."

The book fell at Julie's feet. She stood up. "Get out of my room. I can't stand you either."

"Sure thing, little freak." Alexia stomped out of the room, slamming the door. "I hate this family."

"You're the freak!" shouted Julie.

Alexia's door slammed.

"Julie?" Bean walked into their room and stood next to Julie's desk. "Why are you crying?"

"It's okay. It's my fault." Julie put one arm around her brother. Why did Alexia have to make so much trouble all the time? Julie swallowed hard around the lump in her throat. If only she hadn't forgotten the message. She was so stupid. She looked at Bean, rubbing his eyes.

"It's okay, Julie." Bean patted Julie's back. "I love you."

Julie gave her brother a quick squeeze. "Thanks, Beano."

Nine

FRIDAY. MRS. SPIT would be back, and Julie still didn't have her "poor work" papers signed. She also hadn't copied the spelling words or written the paper about playing with marbles in school. A lot of unfinished work had piled up. Julie's stomach tightened into knots as she walked into the kitchen for breakfast. Maybe Ms. Eddie had forgotten to leave the note about the marble assignment and spelling words for Mrs. Spattelli.

By the time they had started dinner last night, Mom was home. Alexia was still in her room, and Mom told her to come to the table even if she wasn't eating. Bean said Alexia made Julie cry, and Alexia told him to shut up and mind his business, which made Dad yell. Alexia stomped away from the table. Then Mom said Dad should be eating something healthier than cheeseburgers, and they both got mad.

After dinner, Julie had let Bean make a kite picture with her paper scraps while she finished Glenda's card. Julie didn't want to disturb Mom after the scene at dinner, so she found some sparkly thin ribbon in the hallway closet Mom called the junk closet. It looked perfect hanging down the side like streamers. Inside, Julie wrote: "Hoppy birdthay. Love, Julie."

Julie walked to school, kicking a stone all the way. She liked to scrape the rubber toe of her high-tops across the asphalt. They were Alexia's old ones and Julie loved to wear them. Alexia wore platform shoes now. Julie thought they looked dumb.

The hill they lived on was so steep, it was harder walking down than up. When Julie was Bean's age, Dad had to take her to the playground to ride her bike because it was impossible to learn how to ride on such a big slope. They practiced over and over, with Dad holding her up, until finally one time she felt him let go, and instead of falling, she just kept pedaling, going and going like she was free. Now her bike was too small for her. Dad said they couldn't afford a new one right now. She gave her old bike to Bean, but how would he learn to ride if Dad wasn't supposed to do heavy work? Julie could still feel his strong arms holding her up just like it was nothing. How could someone so strong have a heart that just stopped?

With Mrs. Spattelli back, the class was quiet. What a difference from having a substitute. Everyone knew the Spit meant business. There was a rumor that once she had made a boy come in on Saturdays for a whole month to wash her car, clean the school toilets, and wash the floors because he wrote a bad word in chalk dust on the blackboard. Alexia said that rumor was going around even when she had the Spit.

Flop! A folded piece of paper landed on Julie's desk. She looked up. Abby was headed toward the pencil sharpener. She had taken a detour past Julie's desk. When she was sure Mrs. Spit wasn't looking, Julie opened the paper. Gosh! Did Abby have to write a book? The note filled the whole notebook page and part of the back. Julie mouthed the words to herself: "can't wait." The next word was long. She sounded it out: "un-tilt-on-ight." What the heck? What was that word? Untiltonight? She jumped ahead. "My mom can drive to the party." Great! Julie refolded the note and stuck it in her desk. She looked over her shoulder and waved to Abby, who was back at her seat. Abby waved her pencil.

"Julie."

She looked up. Mrs. Spattelli must have seen the note after all.

"Please come up to my desk."

Sighing, she stood up and walked to the teacher's desk. She stood with her back to the class, but she knew everyone was staring, drilling little holes in her back with their eyes.

Mrs. Spattelli looked down at her grade book, then up over the frames of her glasses. "Do you have some papers signed for me?"

"No, I forgot."

"Have your parents seen the papers?"

"Yes," Julie lied. "I just forgot to bring them."

"I see," the teacher said. "If I don't have them back, corrected and signed, on Monday, I will have to call your parents and have another talk."

Julie crossed her arms over her chest and stared

straight ahead like she didn't care what the Spit did.

"By the way," Mrs. Spattelli continued, "how is your father? I know he had some health problems last fall."

"Fine," Julie mumbled.

Mrs. Spattelli stared at Julie over the tops of her glasses with her eyebrows raised like she was expecting something. "Well, good."

Yeah, sure, Julie thought. What a witch. Mrs. Spit didn't care about her father. All she cared about was neat papers and a quiet classroom.

Julie was trembling. Why couldn't the big Spit leave her alone?

Mrs. Spattelli turned and opened the math book that was on top of her desk. At least she wasn't going to ask about the marbles paper. The sub must have forgotten to leave a note.

"You may sit down, Julie. Class, please take out your math homework."

"Wait!"

Mrs. Spattelli looked at her.

Julie's face muscles felt like stone when she tried to speak. "The substitute took my marbles. They're in your top drawer. She said I could have them back after school, but I...," Julie stammered, "she forgot."

Mrs. Spattelli raised her eyebrows. "I didn't see any marbles." She slid the drawer open and bent down to look back inside. Then she opened the other two drawers one at a time and shook her head. "No marbles here, Julie. Are you sure Ms. Eddie put them in my desk?"

Julie nodded. Her marbles were gone.

"Well, perhaps they will turn up. Check your desk. We need to get started on math."

Julie finally managed to speak. "But I . . ." She cleared her throat. "They were there yesterday."

Mrs. Spattelli sighed. She looked up at the class. "Has anyone seen Julie's marbles?"

The class was quiet. Even the rustling of papers stopped.

Then everyone started whispering and talking at once.

"All right, class. If anyone knows anything, come see me later. Julie, sit down."

As Julie walked to her seat, she saw Glenda in the front row whispering to Sara. They looked at Julie without smiling. Julie felt like she was walking through a courtroom. Someone must have taken her marbles out of Mrs. Spattelli's desk. So how come Julie felt like she was the one on trial?

Ten

AFTER MATH, IT was time for art. Everyone was talking about the missing marbles by the time they reached the art room. "Someone's a thief," Brian announced.

"You think someone actually took your marbles?" Abby asked as she sat down at the table next to Julie.

"Well, they aren't in Mrs. Spattelli's desk," Julie told her.

"Who would take them?"

Julie shrugged. She didn't want to talk about it. Today was going from bad to worse. Even the thought of the sleepover tonight didn't cheer her up.

"I'm getting a CD player, so everyone bring music. It will be the best," said Glenda. The party was all she could talk about, even in art class in front of all the kids who weren't invited.

Mr. Nelson gave everyone a lump of clay and showed them how to work it with their fingers to make a pinch pot. Julie worked on her clay. Today she couldn't get the smooth gray lump to do what she wanted it to. Why would someone take her marbles? Brian and Nate were the only ones who really liked the game. But even though he was a tease, Julie couldn't see Brian actually stealing. Nate either. She sighed, then rolled her clay into one big ball, brought her fist down, and pounded it flat. That's all she had to hand in by the time art was over, a round flat piece of clay with the side of her fist printed in it.

Back in the classroom after art, Mrs. Spit was at the board with her back to the class. Brian stopped at Julie's desk on the way to his seat. He bounced his pencil eraser against Julie's head.

She leaned out of his reach.

"Hey," Brian said, "still missing your marbles?" He

twirled his finger at the side of his head and raised his eyebrows.

Julie glared at him. "Cut that out," she hissed.

Brian flipped his pencil up in the air, caught it, and gave her a big fake grin. Then he started to strut to his seat like the dumb clown he was. For all Julie knew, Brian did have her marbles. In a flash, Julie stuck her foot out and caught Brian's right leg just as he passed her.

"Awk!" Brian screeched like a bird. His desk scraped across the floor as he stumbled into it. Julie looked straight ahead.

Mrs. Spattelli turned from the blackboard. "Brian? What is going on back there? Please stand up and straighten your desk."

Julie heard Brian drag his desk back into position. Mrs. Spattelli was peering over her glasses at Brian. Julie sat with her hands folded on the desk, practically holding her breath.

"Well, Brian? What happened? Could you please explain this disruption to the class?"

"Julie tripped me."

Mrs. Spattelli's eyebrows shot up.

"Julie, did you trip Brian?"

"It—it was an accident." Her voice cracked and her face got hot.

Finally Mrs. Spattelli said, "Well, sit up and keep your hands and feet to yourself. And Brian, you watch where you are going." She turned back to the board. Julie let out a long breath, but her mouth was dry and her stomach was in knots. It was impossible to tell what Mrs. Spattelli really thought. Everyone said she had eyes in the back of her head. Did she know Julie had tripped Brian on purpose? Who cared? He deserved it. Brian wasn't going to tell, and Julie was fed up with his tapping and noise and goofing around.

Eleven

"I DON'T BELIEVE I got a B on the social studies unit test. It counts twice." Glenda moaned.

They were sitting on the steps to the fourth- and fifth-grade entrance after lunch. Glenda had shooed all the little kids away, like she owned the place. Now she was being so theatrical, it made Julie sick. Heck, what was Glenda complaining about anyway? Julie had studied all night for that test last week, and all she had to show for her work was a D+.

"I'm going to see if I can get Spattelli to change it to an A. I could do some extra credit," Glenda said.

Gosh! Why was she so upset? Glenda and Abby

always got A's, and Julie could bet they never had to study. Julie would give anything for Glenda's B. She felt miserable. Sara didn't look so happy either. She wasn't saying anything, just wiping her nose and rubbing her eyes like she was crying or something.

"I saw the Brain's paper when I passed them back," Glenda confided. "She got an A++. Mrs. Spattelli loves her to death."

"My dad gives me a dollar for every A," Abby told them. "I probably would have gotten three dollars for an A++."

Abby'd be rich if she were the Brain, Julie thought.

"Let's clap," Glenda said, suddenly grabbing Abby by the wrist and pulling her away from the group. They started clapping with each other and singing "Down, down, baby. Down by the roller coaster." Between claps, they both spun around.

"Want to play?" Sara asked Julie.

"No, thanks," Julie said. She didn't really feel like clapping hands with Sara when she was holding a gross Kleenex that looked like she had been using it for a week. Julie didn't feel like playing, period. She felt hot and her stomach ached. She leaned against the brick wall and watched Abby and Glenda.

Marlene leaned against the wall nearby, but Sara didn't ask her to play. She just wandered off, sniffing.

When Glenda and Abby stopped, they gave each other a high five and giggled. Show-offs, Julie thought. Abby was getting to be as annoying as Glenda.

The girls finished a second round of "Down, down, baby" and fell against the wall, giggling some more. Julie didn't see what was so funny. Sometimes she wondered if Abby was still her best friend. Now that Abby was hanging out with Glenda, it seemed like Julie was losing her. Just like she had lost her marbles. A real loser, Julie thought. That's what she was. That's probably what Abby thought, too.

Julie stopped watching the girls and stared down at her high-tops. They were supposed to be white, but now they looked practically brown, and there was a hole starting at the little toe on her left foot. She bent over to pick at it. When she straightened up again, she was startled to see that Marlene had moved over so close to her, they were almost touching elbows. She looked back down. Marlene wore brown leather shoe boots. The only holes in them were for the laces.

"Well?" Julie said.

Marlene looked out at the other girls playing on

the blacktop before she answered. Then she finally asked in a quiet voice, "Do you really think someone stole your marbles?"

"So what else could have happened to them?" Julie shot back. Why was Marlene even talking to her anyway? "What do you want from me?" she sighed.

Marlene rocked back and forth against the brick wall. "I thought you could teach me how to play marbles."

Julie kept looking at her high-tops, but she could feel the Brain staring at her now. What a weirdo. "There's nothing to teach. You just play marbles." Julie looked over at Marlene and stared back hard. "Besides, I don't have my marbles, remember?"

Marlene looked away.

The bell rang for the end of lunch period. Julie pushed herself away from the wall and walked quickly past Marlene, around the corner of the building, back to their classroom. Right. Like the Brain didn't know how to play marbles. Like she couldn't figure it out. It was almost like she was trying to be friends or something. Just what Julie needed, the Brain for a friend.

Back in the classroom, Julie put her head down

on her desk and listened to the rest of the kids come in. Brian was whistling through his teeth and tapping his ruler on his leg.

"Abby, come this way." That was Glenda's bossy voice. Julie raised her head to see Abby follow Glenda around the room to her desk. Glenda sat down and said, "Bye, Ab." Abby looked over at Julie and raised her eyebrows. Abby was still her friend. Julie remembered the note under her desk. It was long. Abby had spent a long time writing it. Maybe it would make her feel better, Julie thought, if she could read it. She stuck her hand into her cubby to find the note, but what she felt made her sit up straight and stare ahead. Her marbles were right there inside her desk.

Twelve

THE LAST KIDS straggled into the room. Mrs. Spattelli followed them in. Julie felt hot. Maybe she had made a mistake. But she knew she hadn't. This was weird. She knew those marbles hadn't been there this morning. Her spine felt prickly when she thought about someone messing in her desk. If Mrs. Spattelli saw the marbles now, she'd think Julie was a liar.

Julie leaned over and peeked inside. It was hard to see, but her red-and-green marble pouch was definitely perched on top of her social studies book. Slowly she reached her hand inside. As quietly as possible she slid her spelling workbook from the bottom of the pile and placed it over the marbles. At least it hid them for now until she figured out what to do. Other desks squeaked and papers rustled as everyone got ready for language arts, pulling papers and books out of their cubbies.

"Can I get a drink of water?" Brian called out. "Mrs. Spattelli, I'm dying of thirst."

"Brian, it is March and you still haven't learned to raise your hand. No, you may not get a drink of water. You should have done that before coming into the room. It's time to get to work."

Mrs. Spattelli stood up. "Today we are going to start a composition. You can begin it in class now, think about it over the weekend, and finish the rough draft during language arts next week. The title of your composition will be 'One Thing I'm Good At.' Remember to use sentences and paragraphs, each with a main idea."

"How long does it have to be?" Matthew asked.

"It should fill at least two sides of a notebook page, or one full page if you are doing the final draft on the computer."

Several kids groaned.

"That's enough noise. I'm sure you are all good at

something and can take more than a page to tell me about it. Now get started. Jot down ideas and make notes. Think about what you like to do. I know you are all good at many things, but consider the title and stick to only one topic."

Julie put her head down on top of her language arts notebook. How was she going to fill a whole page? There wasn't anything she was good at. Not one thing. Finally she lifted her head and began to write: "I hate school. I hate school. I hate school." By the time the final bell rang, she had filled a whole page.

As Julie trudged up the hill toward home, she thought about the language arts assignment. Writing "I hate school" thirty-six times had made her feel better, but she sure couldn't hand in that paper. What the heck, maybe she just wouldn't do the assignment at all.

One block up and she was on Main Street. She stopped to catch her breath. Turning right would take you into town. Julie wasn't allowed to hang out in town. Left took you down to the river. Julie could see a strip of the muddy brown water between the buildings. She watched a tugboat push a barge piled with coal until they were blocked from sight by the old Schiller factory.

As she turned back to the hill, a car came from town and pulled over at the curve. Someone got out, slammed the door, and waved thank-you. Alexia! That was her denim jacket with the yin/yang painted on the back. They could walk up the hill together. A puff of smoke billowed from the girl's head. She was still facing away from Julie as she brought her hand out and flicked ashes into the street, but Julie knew that jacket. She had watched Alexia paint the design on herself.

Abruptly Julie turned and walked up the hill as fast as she could. Alexia smoking? Mom would kill her. And what about Dad? He'd have a fit. She'd never seen him smoke, but the doctor said that smoking when he was younger had probably helped cause his heart problem. Alexia knew it, too.

She wanted to be wrong. Maybe the person who got out of the car wasn't her sister.

"Julie! Hey! Wait up."

Julie kept walking like she didn't hear her sister's voice. She had enough of her own problems. Mrs.

Spit was going to call her parents if those papers weren't signed by Monday. Her missing marbles had shown up in her desk and she had a dumb essay to write. She didn't need a stupid sister with a butt habit to make things worse.

Thirteen

AT LEAST GLENDA'S party would get her out of the house, Julie thought as she got ready. The door-bell rang, and she asked Bean to let Abby in and tell her she'd be right down.

Julie was juggling her sleeping bag, pillow, gift, and overnight bag as she came down the stairs.

"Julie!" Abby exclaimed as she stepped inside the front door. "What's the sleeping bag for?"

"Aren't we supposed to bring sleeping bags?" Julie dumped everything at the bottom of the stairs in front of the door.

"This *isn't* a sleepover." Abby sounded annoyed.

"It's not?" Julie was confused. "But I thought . . ."

"It's a *swim* party. Didn't you read the invitation? And my note. I told you we could wear our matching suits."

"Sure," Julie mumbled. "I just thought . . . I mean, I forgot."

Abby laughed. "How could you forget your swimsuit for a swim party?" She rolled her eyes.

"Hold on. I'll get it." Julie was already halfway back up the stairs.

"Hurry up. My mom is waiting. We'll be late."

Julie fumbled through her top drawer. She was sure the invitation had said sleepover. How dumb could she get? Where was the suit anyway? She hadn't worn it since last summer. She needed a towel, too.

The suit wasn't in the top drawer. Socks, underwear, pajamas. She dumped them all onto the floor. There was her old striped suit, but Abby wanted her to wear the one with blue flowers just like hers. They'd bought them together last year. She pulled open the second drawer, but that just had tops and sweatshirts. She slammed it in.

"Julie, come on."

Julie grabbed the old suit and stuffed it into her swim bag. She grabbed a towel from the linen closet and stuffed that in, too. Forget the nose plugs. She was never going to find those.

"Finally!" Abby was already out the front door. "We'll be the last ones there," she called over her shoulder.

Mom held the door open as Julie left. She had just gotten home from work. She had kicked off her shoes and the bow on the front of her blouse was untied and hanging down. "Everything okay?" She was frowning. Tired, Julie could tell. Mom was always tired now.

"Yep." Julie turned away from her mother. "Except we're late."

"Bye," Mom called, but Julie didn't even wave. She dashed down the walk to the back seat of Mrs. Edwards's car. Nothing was okay. She didn't have her goggles and she'd forgotten her conditioner. She didn't even know if the old bathing suit fit her, and she didn't know why she was going to this dumb party. She fastened her seat belt. Abby was chatting away about how Glenda's dad had rented the whole Edgewood Club pool just for them and there were hardly any kids going. Glenda was soooo mad her mom said no boys.

Julie took a deep breath. She peeked inside her

bag. At least she'd remembered the gift and her card after all the racing around. She settled back into the seat.

Glenda met the girls in the locker room. "Even the Brain got here before you two. I thought you weren't coming."

"Julie thought you were having a sleepover."

"Everyone has a sleepover," Glenda said. "I wanted to be different."

Julie pulled on her swimsuit. The straps cut into her shoulders, but it would have to do.

"You didn't wear the blue suit," Abby groaned when Julie got out of the dressing stall. Then Abby grabbed her towel, turned, and tossed her head as she went out the door to the pool with Glenda.

Out at the pool, everyone was already in the water. "Hurry up. We want to play Marco Polo," Sara sniffed.

Julie held her nose and jumped in the deep end. When she came back up to the top she shook the hair out of her face and frog-kicked over to the other girls.

"We have to play down here," Glenda said. "Because Marlene can't swim in the deep end." Glenda raised her eyebrows. Marlene acted like she didn't hear. She just swam to the wall, held on, and kicked.

"You be it, Glenda," Abby said. "It's your birthday."

They played Marco Polo and water basketball and football, and then Glenda's mom threw weighted colored sticks in the water. Julie got a little address book as a prize for finding the red one. It had the highest number on it. Glenda acted like she was supposed to win just because it was her birthday, so they had to do it over and over again until Glenda got the red stick. She was acting just like a little kid. Even Bean behaved better. Marlene didn't play that game at all.

When it was time for cake, the girls wrapped their towels around themselves and sat at the tables at the edge of the pool.

"Let's open gifts now," Glenda suggested.

"Open mine first." Abby grabbed her gift off the top of the pile. Everyone got up again and crowded around Glenda. Julie waited, holding her gift. She straightened the card, which she had stuck on with a piece of tape.

"Here," she said when Glenda was ready for another present.

The birthday girl opened the card without even

looking at the kite picture. One of the streamers floated to the wet tile floor. She squinted at the writing. "Hoppy birdthay?" She wrinkled up her nose. "Hoppy birdthay," she said and laughed.

Julie felt the heat creep up to her cheeks.

Ruth Ann repeated it. "Hoppy birdthay! That's a good one, Julie." She pulled off the other streamer and tossed it up into the air. It landed, leaving a blue-green smudge on the tile floor.

The girls passed the card around, giggling, as Glenda ripped open her present. Nobody looked at the kite picture, not even Abby.

"Mine's next," Sara said, tossing the rumpled kite card into the pile of wrapping that was growing around Glenda's ankles.

All the work she had put into that card, and no one liked it. All they noticed was that she couldn't spell. Everyone crowded closer around Glenda to admire the denim purse. Julie didn't care if they liked the stupid purse. Unable to hold back the tears, she turned and fled back to the locker room.

The door swished shut behind her. How stupid could she be to write *Hoppy birdthay?* Nothing she did turned out right. Tears flowed silently as Julie stood in front of the mirror by the sink. Her reflection blurred in front of her. Then she let the sobs out. She cried for her ruined card and for her mean friends, and she cried because she was so dumb and because there was nothing she was good at, no matter what Mrs. Spit said.

Fourteen

WITH ANOTHER SWISH, the locker-room door swung open. Before Julie could hide, Marlene stood staring at her.

Julie wiped away the tears. "Leave me alone." She wanted to dive into a stall and stay there until the party was over and she could go home.

Marlene held out the torn, rumpled card. "I like it. I think it's a great picture." She flattened the paper out on the edge of the sink. "Maybe we could fix it with tape."

Julie sniffed and dragged the back of her hand across her eyes. Why couldn't Marlene just go away?

For someone so smart, she sure was dumb. Anyone could see the card was beyond repair. Anger filled the place where the tears came from. She grabbed the card and tore it in half and then in half again. "It was stupid," she said and stuffed it through the swinging lid of the trash can.

Marlene drew in her breath. "But I wanted to keep it."

"Keep it! Why?"

Marlene just stared in that dumb way she had.

Finally she said, "I'm not good at art. I couldn't make anything like that. I can't believe you would just tear it up. If I got that card, I'd frame it. No one ever made anything like that for me."

Julie stared at the Brain. Her hair was braided, and the wet ends stuck out like straw hair on a scarecrow. Suddenly she wanted to laugh. Marlene, the Brain, the teacher's pet and the kid who got A++ on her tests, thought she wasn't good in art. Poor little Marlene.

Julie punched in the swinging lid of the trash can. Three times she hit it, and three times it swung and clattered. The loud noise echoed in the tiled room. "I don't know what you've got to complain about," Julie snapped. "You're the Brain. You're good at everything." She slammed the trash can one more time.

Marlene's mouth fell open and she stared wide-eyed through her glasses.

"I'm good at nothing," Julie spit out, like the words tasted awful. "Nothing but stupid stuff," she said more softly. "Art doesn't count."

Marlene didn't answer, and suddenly Julie felt too weak to even stand up. What was she doing standing here talking to the Brain about things she'd never told anyone—not Abby, not even Alexia when they used to talk? She leaned back against the cool tile wall and walked her feet out, sliding down into a sitting position. Marlene slid down the opposite wall, facing Julie with outstretched legs. Their toes nearly touched.

"Art does count," she said with a crooked smile. "My dad's an artist, but I didn't get any of his genes. My mom says I'm lucky." She sighed. "He's supposed to come to visit this summer. He's going to bring me a painting. But Mom says not to hold my breath. She says he's not dependable." Suddenly Marlene wasn't smiling anymore.

Julie had never heard the Brain talk so much at one time, unless she was answering questions in class. Her dad was an artist? She hadn't known that. Come to think of it, she didn't know anything about the Brain except that she was smart and weird.

"Where is your dad?"

"He lives in an artist's colony in New Mexico. My parents are divorced."

"Oh." Why was Marlene telling her all this private stuff about her dad? Julie never told anyone anything about her dad, that he had a heart attack. Abby knew, but they never talked about it. Julie never even said the words *heart attack*. She felt as if telling someone would make her dad's heart problems more real. If she didn't talk about it, she could pretend there was nothing to worry about. But it'd be hard to pretend your dad didn't live in New Mexico.

"My dad used to be a fireman," she said all of a sudden.

The locker-room door popped open. Glenda's mom stuck her head in. "You girls coming out for cake?"

Julie stood up. Her legs were stiff. "Sure." She hoped Mrs. Bradley didn't know she'd been crying.

Marlene got up, too, but didn't say anything.

"Come and get it." The door swooshed closed again. Julie looked in the mirror.

"You don't look like you've been crying," Marlene said behind her. "But my mom says cold water helps."

Julie's smile was shaky. "I'm okay. Thanks," she mumbled. "Come on, let's go." She pushed open the door.

Marlene grabbed her arm. "Julie, wait."

Now what? Julie waited, one arm holding the door open.

"I took your marbles out of Mrs. Spattelli's desk." The words came out in a rush.

Julie let go of the door. It swung shut and banged against her shoulder, but the shock of the door hitting her was nothing compared to the surprise Marlene's words had given her.

"You?"

"Don't be mad," Marlene said. "I put them back in your desk. You must have seen them."

"You?" Julie asked again.

Suddenly the door flew open once more. It was Glenda. "Sorry to break up the private party. My mom says we can't sing 'Happy Birthday' until you two get out here."

Julie followed Glenda out the door without saying a word. Marlene trailed behind them.

"Julie has a new best friend," Glenda announced to Abby as they approached the party tables. Both girls stared at her, but Julie hardly noticed. Did she have a new friend? Why else would Marlene say she liked the card and tell her all that stuff about her parents? Marlene was the only one who liked her card, and Julie had almost told her about Dad's heart attack. But why would Marlene take her marbles? Everyone sang "Happy Birthday," but Julie barely mouthed the words. She wished she knew what was going on with Marlene.

Fifteen

SUNDAY MORNING, JULIE sat squeezed together with Bean on the same chair in front of the white computer screen. She was teaching him how to type *Benjamin Dorinsky*. Bean used one finger to punch the letters Julie spelled for him. He had to search for each one for so long that Julie had to hold herself back from doing it for him. She smiled, watching his little tongue poke out between his teeth as he concentrated. Poor Bean, Julie thought. He had two long names that were never going to fit on one line of first-grade writing paper. Parents should think of those things when they named a kid.

"*Y!*" Bean shouted as he stabbed the last key. "I did it!"

"Great, Bean. Now we'll print it, and you can copy your name five times for practice."

"Five?" Bean asked, holding up the outstretched fingers of his right hand in front of his face. He peeked between his fingers and smiled at Julie.

A fresh sheet of paper floated out of the printer with Bean's full name in neat bold letters, and Julie handed it to her brother. "If you do a good job, you get a treat. Now let me get my homework done. You can work at the kitchen table."

"A real treat?" Bean made his eyes big in anticipation.

"If you finish all five and let me finish my work." Julie had a peanut butter cup in the favor bag from Glenda's party up on her desk. Peanut butter cups were Bean's favorite.

Bean galloped into the kitchen as Julie hit backspace and watched Bean's name disappear from the screen without a trace. In science she learned everything was either a solid, a liquid, or a gas. She'd even made up a game where she and Bean went around the house naming things solid, liquid, or gas. But what were the computer letters on a screen?

Another one of those dumb things no one else but her ever thought about. Julie sighed. She had bigger problems to worry about, but finally she'd figured out how to take care of them.

It was so easy, Julie didn't know why she hadn't thought of the solution sooner. She had to have the papers signed by Monday. If she told Dad and Mom now, they would both worry and get upset and probably argue and it would be her fault.

But Julie didn't have to show her parents all those "poor work" papers. She was going to write a note to Mrs. Spattelli herself. She was going to write a note to her on the computer, as if it was from Mom and Dad, and the evidence would disappear with the letters on the screen.

She would hand it in tomorrow and Mrs. Spattelli would be happy and Mom and Dad never had to know. This would fix everything.

"Dear Mrs. Spattelli," she wrote, carefully copying her teacher's name off of one of the papers. "Please exkuse Julie for not reterning all the poor werk paphers. She shooed them to us but her brother tride to eat them."

Julie remembered that they had had to tell how old their brothers and sisters were at the beginning of school. Mrs. Spit would know Bean was too old to eat homework. She deleted that part and changed it to "her yunger brother flushed them down the toylet and mad a mes." Julie read the letter to herself. Then she added, "Yours trulie, Mr. and Mrs. Dorinsky." She hit print, and sat back in the chair with her arms crossed over her chest. Now all she had to do was write that stupid paper about what she was good at. She'd asked Dad, and he said she was good at everything. Right. Like he really thought she could do anything she wanted if she really tried.

Mom would probably say something like taking out the trash or setting the table and then ask her to do it. Alexia would say she was good at nothing, and for once, her older sister would be right. She still had five days to think of something.

"Hey." Julie almost jumped out of her seat. "I need to use the computer." Alexia stood in the doorway with an armload of books.

Julie stood up, blocking her sister's view of the computer screen. She quickly hit backspace, holding her finger on the key as she turned toward her sister. "I was here first."

"I have homework, and Dad says to do it now

'cause he needs the computer later."

"Well, I have homework, too." Julie folded her arms across her chest and stuck her chin out.

"Sorry, babe, age takes precedence." Alexia dropped her books onto the computer table and elbowed Julie out of the way. "What kind of homework do you need the computer for anyway?" She reached across Julie toward the printer, where Julie's letter stuck out like a tongue.

Julie grabbed the letter and held it behind her back, stepping out of Alexia's reach. "None of your business."

"Hey." Alexia held up both hands. "No problem. I don't care what you're doing. Just get out of here so I can get my work done."

Alexia always thought she was the boss. Julie could fix that. "Leave me alone," she spit out, "or I'll tell Mom and Dad you're smoking. I saw you."

For a split second Alexia looked surprised. "You did not!"

"Did too," Julie said.

Alexia grabbed her arm and squeezed. It hurt. "You better not tell, you little freak."

Julie pulled away and stared at her sister. Neither

of them said a word. Alexia looked mean and ugly. Julie wanted to hit her. She wanted to hit her and cry at the same time. That's what her sister wanted, to make her cry. But Julie wasn't going to, not in front of Alexia. Let her have the stupid computer. She was finished with her letter anyway. All she wanted was to get away from her sister.

Julie grabbed her "poor work" papers and raced up the stairs, rubbing her arm where Alexia had twisted it. When she reached her room, she threw herself on the bed and tried to slow her breathing. What had happened to Alexia? Abby was always saying how great it must be to have an older sister. Like she knew. Sure, before Alexia went to high school, they used to talk about school and stuff. Now they just fought all the time. All Alexia ever did was make mean jokes or tell her to get lost.

"Julie?" Bean was standing at the foot of the bed holding his paper out for her to see. She forgot she had to check his work. She was too angry right now. "Go away, Bean!" she yelled. "Just get lost."

"It's my room too," Bean said.

"No it isn't. Leave me alone." Julie's voice cracked.

"Julie? What about my treat?"

"Go away, Bean. There is no treat. I lied," she screamed and turned her back on him. She heard her brother leave. "And don't come back," she whispered. Julie's body shook with sobs as she lay curled up on her bed, still holding her papers and the letter.

Sixteen

ON MONDAY MORNING the letter to her teacher was folded neatly in Julie's backpack. The "poor work" papers were stuffed in the bottom of her desk drawer. She hadn't decided how to get rid of them yet. She walked slowly down the steep hill to school and thought about her plan. She felt miserable. When she'd read the note this morning, it didn't look right. It looked too short. Two little lines on the top of a full sheet of paper. Julie's stomach twisted into knots. Maybe Mrs. Spattelli would forget again, and Julie wouldn't have to give her the fake letter after all.

No matter how much she dragged her feet, it seemed to Julie that she still got to school early. She walked across the playground toward the front of the school. Most of the kids hadn't even lined up yet. Abby, Glenda, Sara, and Ruth Ann were huddled in a little circle on the blacktop. Marlene was nowhere around, which was fine with her.

Julie's stomach flip-flopped again as she entered the classroom. Marlene was up at Mrs. Spattelli's desk. That's why she wasn't out on the playground.

Julie heard Mrs. Spattelli tell Marlene to go hang up her coat and sit down. Marlene turned around and looked straight at Julie. She smiled and waved. Julie pretended she didn't notice and waited for Mrs. Spattelli to call her up to her desk and ask for her corrected homework. How had she gotten in such a mess? The sunny March day outside was a blur. Shoot. She blinked hard. That's all she needed was to start crying here in school, sitting in front of loudmouth Brian, with Marlene staring at her from across the room.

Julie fought the tears until her head ached, but she managed to get through the morning without breaking down. It was all business as usual. Maybe Mrs. Spattelli really had forgotten about everything.

Finally it was lunchtime. Mrs. Spattelli dismissed them one row at a time to get lunches and line up for the cafeteria, but before Julie made it to the door, she heard her teacher's raspy voice from the front of the room. "Julie, could you please come see me before going to lunch?" She said it like a question, but Julie knew it was an order.

She stopped in her tracks, stomach tightening. By the time she got to the front of the room, everyone else was in line. Mrs. Spattelli told the class to go ahead quietly. Then she stared at Julie. "Marlene came to me this morning and told me that she was the one who took the marbles out of my desk. She said it wasn't your fault that they fell all over the floor, and she didn't think the substitute should have taken them."

Julie's face was on fire to the tips of her ears. She just stared back at her teacher.

"Marlene said she put the marbles back in your desk. Is that true?"

Julie nodded.

"Well, I explained to Marlene that what she did was wrong. She should have left the marbles where they were and perhaps come to me when I got back, but under the circumstances and since I wasn't here, we'll just forget about all this."

Julie nodded again. She held her breath and waited to see what would come next.

Mrs. Spattelli still stared at her, but she looked like she was thinking of something else. Finally she reached out and touched Julie on the shoulder. Julie flinched.

Mrs. Spattelli sighed and dropped her hand. "Go eat your lunch," she said.

Julie turned around and walked quickly out of the room. The rubber soles of Alexia's old high-tops squeaked on the polished tile floor with every step.

Seventeen

BY THE TIME Julie got to the cafeteria, most of the kids from her class were already outside for recess. She sat by herself and picked at her sandwich. The next class hadn't come in yet, and the cafeteria ladies were looking at her.

Maybe Marlene wasn't a creep after all. Why did Julie think it in the first place? Because everything else was such a mess and she felt like a creep herself, that's why. One problem was solved, but the marbles were nothing. If only the rest would just go away as easily. She should have given Mrs. Spattelli the fake letter when she had the chance. Standing up, she bunched her sandwich in the waxed paper and threw it all in the trash.

Outside it was beautiful. The sunshine flowed over Julie as soon as she stepped through the door. Kids' jackets and sweatshirts were all over the steps and ground. Everyone was running wild.

"Got your marbles?" The voice startled her. It was Marlene. She was smiling.

"What do you want?" Julie blurted out. She felt tense and guilty, like Marlene knew about her phony letter. "Just because you told Mrs. Spattelli about the marbles, you think we're friends?"

Marlene's smile disappeared. She looked surprised. Her mouth made a silly little O shape. And then suddenly, as if she had been touched by a magic wand, she changed back to the old Marlene, turning half away from Julie, arms hanging like she didn't know what to do with them. Like she was there but not there, like she wanted to sink into the blacktop.

Julie stared at the Brain, feeling powerful, like the mean witch who held the wand. Like Glenda, who could make anyone feel miserable. It made her mad. "Hey," she yelled, "why do you do that? You're the Brain. Why do you act so dumb?" Julie was practically screaming now.

Marlene turned back toward Julie. Her mouth was open again, but she didn't look so much like she wanted to disappear.

"Why don't you tell me I'm a jerk? Tell me you're the only one who didn't laugh at my card?" Julie spoke in a hiss now. She knew what she wanted. "Go ahead, say it." She took a step closer to the girl in front of her.

"But you're not a jerk, Julie," Marlene said simply, just like a little kid. Like the Bean would say it.

"Look," Julie said. "Say it and I'll . . . I'll . . . I'll teach you how to play marbles."

Marlene looked at her like she was crazy, but she wasn't disappearing now. She looked interested.

"Try it one word at a time," Julie said. "You."

"You," Marlene repeated.

"Are."

"Are."

"Louder," Julie ordered.

"Louder," Marlene said, her lips forming the tiniest of smiles.

"A," Julie continued, holding back a giggle.

"A," Marlene said. And then, before Julie could say it, she added, giggling, "Jerk!"

"Jerk!" Julie shouted and then burst out laughing.

Julie pointed at Marlene. "Dummy," she said, still laughing.

Marlene pointed back, giggling so she could barely speak. "Brain!" she said.

Startled, Julie couldn't think of anything else to say. "Double Brain." She snickered.

Marlene's laughter echoed Julie's.

The bell rang. They looked at each other and laughed some more. Julie's stomach began to hurt. She took a deep breath to calm herself down.

"Are you still going to teach me marbles?" Marlene choked on a giggle.

"Why do you want me to teach you?" Julie asked. "Anybody can play marbles."

"Because you're a good teacher," Marlene said. They were both in control now.

"How do you know?"

"I saw you teaching the other kids. You made it look like fun."

"Maybe tomorrow," Julie said. She followed Marlene into the school. "Hey," she said just before they got to their classroom. Marlene turned around. "When did you do it?"

"What?" Marlene asked.

"Take the marbles."

"Oh." Marlene lowered her eyes. "Right after the spelling bee. When everyone went to lunch." She looked back up at Julie. "I was going to give them to you at recess, but there wasn't a good time and then we came back in and I still had the marbles. I didn't know what to do with them. When Mrs. Spattelli came back and everyone was talking about a thief, I got scared. I finally put them in your desk at lunchtime. I got lucky and Mrs. Spattelli wasn't in the room." Marlene smiled again crookedly. "I was trying to help."

"Yeah," Julie said. "Thanks."

Marlene nodded, smiling broadly now. Julie thought she was pretty when she smiled. She walked behind Marlene and admired her shiny dark brown hair, which was woven into neat braids. Maybe, Julie thought, she could braid her hair like that. Maybe she'd get rid of the old high-tops, too, and get shoe boots, like Marlene's.

Eighteen

THAT AFTERNOON JULIE walked home from school quickly. Mrs. Spattelli still hadn't asked for the papers. Julie figured it was an omen. She'd been given one more chance to make her plan work. She would write a better letter, make it longer, and then even if her teacher forgot to ask, she would give it to her.

It was warm, but Julie walked fast. She carried her jacket over her arm. Two more telephone poles and she would be at the top of the hill where her street turned off. Twenty-five steps between poles. Julie had counted once. Fifty more steps: 47, 48, 49, 50, she counted. She took a giant step to reach the last pole on 50 and turned the corner.

Something was wrong. One block down, almost to the corner, there were people standing around. There was a police car and a fire engine and an ambulance. They all had flashing lights. Julie strained to see. Maybe they were in front of old Mrs. Staymore's house. Once the ambulance had come because Mrs. Staymore broke her hip. No. The ambulance was in front of her own house. Julie kept walking, not slow or fast. She just kept moving, trying to think of something else: 61, 62, 63. Counting didn't help. The ambulance was in front of her house, just like she had imagined all those times she heard a siren. As Julie drew closer, she could see her mother and Bean. And then she could see Dad. He was tied down on a stretcher, and there was a big kind of tank next to him and two paramedics leaning over him.

Even though she was staring right at it, it wasn't real. It was like a movie—the same picture she had played in her mind hundreds of times. But when Julie imagined this, she never imagined far enough to see if her father had died. Now it was happening right in front of her, and Julie didn't know the answer. It was the one thing she couldn't imagine. If her father died, if his heart really stopped for good, how would it be? Julie caught her breath. It felt like her own heart would stop. She started running then. "Daddy!" she yelled. "Daddy." The tears streamed down her face.

"Julie. Sweetheart. Julie." Somebody grabbed Julie and tried to hold her like a trap. "Julie, it's okay. Julie, stop." Mom was squeezing her, crushing her, holding her. "He's alive! Julie!"

"Julie," Bean said. He grabbed Julie's leg. "I called 911, like you said. The mens came and woke Daddy up."

Julie tried to pat Bean on the back. They were all tangled up together, Mom and Julie and Bean. Julie could hear voices crackling over the police radio. She could see Dad out of the corner of one eye. He was strapped to the stretcher with a tube coming out of a mask over his face.

Julie didn't want to look. She wanted to stay wrapped up in Mom's arms. But Mom was letting go, stepping back. "They are taking him to the hospital," she said. "Let me talk to the paramedics."

Julie followed slowly, holding on to Bean's little hand. They were picking Dad up now, slowly raising him into the truck. His head was propped up just a little, and Julie could see his face, gray like the mask over his nose and mouth, a face like Dad's but not Dad's. The person on the stretcher moved one hand from under the blankets and raised it just a little. He made a tiny waving motion at her. Big tears ran down her face. She watched Mom talk to the ambulance driver. Mom wasn't crying. She looked serious, like she was taking care of business. It made Julie feel better. She kept her eyes on Mom.

The police car and the fire truck were gone. Julie hadn't even seen them leave. Now the ambulance was pulling away from the curb, and Mom turned to Julie and Bean. "I have to go to the hospital," she said. "I don't know what time I'll be home. Alexia should be here soon. Tell her I'll call as soon as I can."

Julie and Bean watched Mom leave. Julie wanted to run to her and tell her not to go, but she couldn't move.

Bean tugged on her arm. His face was streaked where he had wiped his tears with dirty fingers. "Is Daddy going to die, Julie?" A sob shook his little body.

"No, Bean. Dad will be home soon. He was last time. Remember?" Julie wished saying it would make it true. She gave Bean a hug. "Come on, let's go in."

"Julie!" Alexia was running down the street toward them. Her purse and her jacket were flying out to the side. She stopped in front of Julie and Bean. "I saw an ambulance and then Mom's car. I waved, but she didn't see me." She took a deep breath. "What are you doing outside?" Alexia looked hard at Bean and then Julie, like they were guilty of something.

They didn't have a chance to answer.

"Julie, where's Dad?" She was practically screaming now.

"They took him to the hospital," Julie told her sister. "Dad's okay. Mom's going to call as soon as she can."

Alexia slumped onto the steps. "I knew this was going to happen." She said it like she was angry. Like she thought it was Dad's fault.

"I called 911," Bean told her. Alexia didn't say anything, and Julie felt like she didn't have the energy to even talk to her.

"Come on. Let's get inside where we can hear the phone," Julie said, leading Bean into the house. Alexia just sat where she was.

Julie asked Bean if he wanted a snack, but he wasn't hungry. Julie couldn't eat either. She didn't even feel like watching TV. Finally Alexia came in from the front steps and picked up the phone. "I have to call Dean," she said as she headed for the stairs.

"Don't make it long. Mom might want to call," said Julie.

Dean was Alexia's new boyfriend. Her sister was lucky to have someone to talk with, Julie thought. It was funny, but the person that Julie wanted to call was Marlene. She wasn't going to, of course, but somehow Julie felt like having your dad live in New Mexico and having your dad in the hospital were kind of the same thing.

Instead of talking on the phone, Julie played checkers with Bean. They did paper, scissors, rock to see who would go first. They had to do it three times because Bean wanted to. Julie didn't care how many times they had to play the dumb game. Playing kept her from thinking about Dad.

Nineteen

MOM CAME HOME with hamburgers for a late dinner and they all ate together. Alexia didn't complain about the meat once. Mom said the doctors had bad news and good news. Dad's heart had started beating irregularly, and that's why he passed out. They said it could happen again, but they were going to put an electrical pacemaker in his body that would help keep his heart beating normally. He could be home in three days.

When they finished eating, Alexia offered to do the dishes without anyone telling her to. Mom had to make some phone calls to her boss.

"I'll clear," Julie said. They were almost finished

when Alexia stopped stacking the dishwasher and looked up. "You know, Julie, if you hadn't taught Bean about 911, Dad could be dead now."

Julie stared at her sister, not sure what to say. "I can't imagine it. Can you?"

Alexia continued without waiting for an answer. Suddenly she threw her arms around Julie and squeezed her tight. Julie hugged her sister back. They stood like that for a few minutes, and Julie could feel her heart pounding, or maybe it was Alexia's. Her sister finally pulled away, wiping her eyes with the back of her hand. She smiled. "We have to stick together," she said.

"Uh-huh." Julie finally found her voice, but she barely knew what to say. "I know." She nodded self-consciously.

"Look," Alexia added, "I want to tell you. I wanted to tell you yesterday but I was too mad. I stopped smoking. I mean, I just wanted to try it. I know it's dumb, and smoking is probably one reason Dad is in such a mess now." She blushed. "I didn't even like it. It burned my nose and I hated the taste."

Julie nodded. "I'm glad." She smiled. "I'm glad you stopped and I'm glad you told me." She shrugged.

There was so much else she wanted to tell her sister about school and Marlene, but she couldn't right now. There were some things she had to do first, and Alexia couldn't help her do them.

"Julie," Mom called from the next room. "Phone."

"Go ahead," Alexia said. "I'm almost finished."

Who would call me? Julie wondered as she went into the dining room, where Mom sat with the phone. Bean was next to her. Mom put her hand over the receiver. "It's a reporter from channel 4 TV," she explained. "They want to do a story. Bean talked to them and told them you taught him how to call the emergency number, so they want to talk to you."

Julie looked at her brother. He nodded, scrunched up his nose, and made a thumbs-up sign to Julie. Mom and Julie both laughed. Then Julie took the phone.

The voice on the other end was friendly. The reporter wanted to know how Julie taught Bean to dial 911 and what gave her the idea. Julie told her how she and Bean would act out emergencies, like a fire or someone getting hurt, and Bean would practice calling 911 on the play phone, like it was a game. Julie told him what to say and had him memorize his name and address.

"The 911 receptionist said that the little guy didn't even cry," the woman told Julie. "He said your brother did better than most adults when they call.

"But," the reporter added, "do you know you're the real hero here? Without your responsible behavior and fine work as a teacher, your dad might not be alive now."

Julie didn't like thinking about her dad's not being alive now, but she was pleased by the idea that she had helped save him. "Thanks," she said.

"Thanks for talking with me. We want to get this story on the late evening news tonight. I told your mom that I'd like to come over to tape an interview with you and Ben. You can say just what you've told me on the phone."

Julie said, "Fine," and the reporter hung up.

The reporter and cameraman came in less than half an hour. They moved some chairs around and pushed the coffee table against the wall. The reporter sat down with Julie and Bean on the couch and began to ask questions. The camera lights made the living room brighter than daytime. Bean kept squinting and Julie saw white spots when she closed her eyes. The reporter said to just pretend the camera wasn't there and act naturally. Julie answered just as she had on the phone, but she didn't feel very natural. Bean seemed totally relaxed as he demonstrated on his little plastic phone how he had called 911.

"Well," Mom said after they left, "we have a couple of real heroes in this family. I am so proud of you two." She grabbed Julie and Bean together in a hug. "But even heroes need a bath." She looked at Bean, who groaned. "And heroes still need to study." Mom looked at Julie. "Any homework?"

Julie nodded. There was some very important work she had to do right away.

Up in her room, Julie pulled all the "poor work" papers and unfinished homework out of her bottom drawer. She pressed out the wrinkles with the palm of her hand and made two neat piles. She took a deep breath and let it out slowly. There weren't so many, really. Six in the "poor work" pile and four in the unfinished homework stack. It didn't seem like such a big deal after all. Julie took the computer letter from her backpack. She was glad she hadn't given it to Mrs. Spattelli today. She folded it in quarters and ripped it up into tiny pieces. She sprinkled the pieces like snow into her trash can.

Mom had finished giving Bean his bath and came into their room to get his pajamas. Julie sat in the tiny circle of light cast by her desk lamp. "Mom," she said in a quiet voice, "I need to show you something."

Mom bent over the two piles of papers. She looked at each one and then stared at Julie. "How long have you had these?"

Julie kept her eyes down and shrugged. She could feel Mom's gaze on her. Finally she looked up. "I forgot some, and then I didn't want to bother you or upset Dad, and I thought I could take care of it myself." Julie's lip began to quiver, but she didn't let herself cry. "I need to bring them in tomorrow, signed."

Mom sighed. "Okay, Julie, but I'm going to write a note to Mrs. Spattelli and tell her I didn't see them until this evening. I'll explain about Dad and tell her as soon as things settle down, I would like to discuss how we can solve some of these problems with her. And, Julie," Mom added, pulling her into a hug, "I want you to know that no matter how busy I am, I still have time to help with your problems. You don't have to worry about upsetting me or Dad. Okay?"

Julie nodded. Tomorrow she would take the papers

to Mrs. Spattelli and hear whatever the teacher had to say about them and her mother's note. She could handle it. Nothing could be as bad as coming around the corner of your street to see your dad on a stretcher getting loaded into an ambulance.

Twenty

JULIE, MOM, ALEXIA, and Bean all stayed up to watch the news Monday night. The reporter did most of the report standing in the 911 operator center, but they showed Bean dialing his phone and Julie explaining how they practiced for an emergency. The best part for Julie was the scene with Dad in his hospital bed. When the reporter asked if he had known Julie had been teaching Bean about emergencies, he said no, but he wasn't at all surprised by his children's heroic behavior.

Julie overslept and was late getting to school on Tuesday. By the time she got to her class, everyone was already seated at their desks. As soon as she walked into the room, Brian, Nate, and some of the other boys started chanting, "Her-o, her-o." Everyone, including Mrs. Spattelli, stood up and clapped.

Then she noticed the big yellow star taped to the top of the blackboard at the front of the room. There was a class picture of Julie taped in the middle, and underneath in big letters it said, CLASS HERO. TV 4 NEWS STAR. WAY TO GO, JULIE.

Julie's face was red hot as she walked to her desk and sat down. Brian started chanting behind her: "Speech, speech." Julie turned around and crossed her eyes at him and then faced front.

"Julie," Mrs. Spattelli said after the class had settled down, "we are all very proud of you and hope your father is doing well."

Julie didn't know what to say, so she just smiled.

Many of her classmates had not seen the late news. They all had lots of questions, so Mrs. Spattelli asked Julie to tell them about what had happened.

"Now," her teacher said after she was finished, "Mr. Esposito would like to see you in the office as soon as possible."

"Oh, man," Brian exclaimed behind her, "glad I'm not no hero."

Julie looked back at him. He had slapped his hand to his forehead and slumped down in his chair.

A few kids laughed.

"Well, Brian, I guess you don't have to worry about that," Mrs. Spattelli said. More kids laughed.

"And Julie doesn't have to worry either. The principal thinks it's a good idea for all the kindergartners and first graders to learn how to call 911 and report an accident or emergency. He's going to ask for Julie's help." Mrs. Spattelli looked at Julie. "You can go see him now."

Julie opened her backpack and took out the pile of "poor work" papers and homework and the note from Mom. She walked to the front of the room. "I was supposed to give you these," she said and handed the papers to her teacher.

Mrs. Spattelli glanced at the papers and then gave her attention back to Julie. "Okay, we'll talk about these later. You go to Mr. Esposito now."

Julie turned to leave. Marlene caught her eye and mouthed, "Congratulations."

"Julie," Abby whispered as she got near the back

of the room. She held up a piece of notebook paper with a blue ribbon drawn on it. There was a big #1 in the center. Julie smiled and headed to the office.

When Julie got back to class, it was perfectly quiet. All the kids had their heads bent reading their workbooks, except for Brian, who was playing with his ruler and a rubber band.

Julie headed for her seat, but Mrs. Spattelli called her up to the front of the room. She pulled up a chair from the reading table and asked Julie to sit down with her at her desk. "I'm glad you finally handed these in," said Mrs. Spattelli. "I was about to call your mother. I'm glad I don't have to bother her. It sounds like things at your house are a little crazy right now."

Julie nodded.

"When things calm down, then I'll talk to your mom. In the meantime, I've looked over your papers, and I think there are some things we can work on to help you. Are you willing to do a little extra work?"

"Yes," Julie said in a quiet voice.

"Good," Mrs. Spattelli said. "We can talk some more at the end of the day. Now go back to your seat and get started on the math assignment on the board."

Julie took out a fresh clean piece of paper and wrote her name neatly at the top in cursive. She put down the date: March 28—the day she was starting over. It felt good.

On the playground after lunch, Marlene showed Julie a new bag of marbles all her own and asked if they could practice together.

Glenda, Abby, Sara, and Ruth Ann came over and stood around watching.

Marlene took aim and flicked her thumb at a green and white shooter. It tapped a red cat's-eye marble and knocked it right into the circle Julie had drawn on the ground and stayed there without rolling out.

"See, it's easy," Julie told her. "Try to get them all in."

"Hey," Glenda sneered, "I thought the Brain was only good at brainy things." She laughed, but no one else seemed to think she was funny. Julie made a face at Marlene and took her turn.

Brian and Nate wandered over to the group and watched as Marlene shot again. "Want to have a chance to win your shooter back?" Brian asked just as the bell rang. Julie and Marlene scrambled to pick up all the marbles.

"Sure," Julie said. "How about on Friday? Marlene is going to play for me."

"All right!" Brian and Nate slapped each other five.

"Julie!" Marlene hissed. "I can't."

"Sure you can," Julie told her. "Didn't you say I was a good teacher?"

"Yeah, but maybe I'm not such a good student."

Julie laughed. "The Brain not a good student? Just wait until Friday, we'll kill those guys."

Back in the room Mrs. Spattelli reminded the class that they had a writing assignment due soon. The first draft was due tomorrow, so they could use the afternoon for writing workshop and anyone who was ready could get into groups and read to each other. A few kids got up to sit together at the reading table. Of course Abby and Glenda were there, but Julie didn't even care. Now she had a great idea to write about and she couldn't wait to get going.

At the top of the paper she wrote: "One Thing I'm Good At." Then she made two dots, for a colon, and wrote TEACHING. Underneath Julie wrote: "For Bean, the best learner ever." Just like they did in real books. For once she felt good about writing a paper. This was one assignment Julie knew wouldn't need to be signed, but already she couldn't wait to show Mom and Dad—and maybe even Alexia.

Karen Lynn Williams

When Karen Lynn Williams was growing up in New Haven, Connecticut, her dream was to become the youngest novelist ever. At the age of ten, she formed a writing group with some of her friends. They would lounge around on pillows and in old stuffed chairs in her basement and write for hours. When Karen hadn't produced the hoped-for novel by the age of twelve, she gave up on her dream of early publication, but not on writing. Although it took longer than she initially thought it would, eventually Karen became the award-winning author of such books as *Baseball and Butterflies* (a novel) and *Galimoto* and *Painted Dreams,* both picture books illustrated by Catherine Stock.

Karen Lynn Williams lives with her husband, Steven, and their children, Peter, Christopher, Rachel, and Jonathan, in Pittsburgh, Pennsylvania.